D0221416

Director of the World and Other Stories

DIRECTOR OF THE WORLD

& OTHER STORIES

JANE McCAFFERTY

UNIVERSITY OF PITTSBURGH PRESS

Pittsburgh and London

Published by the University of Pittsburgh Press, Pittsburgh, Pa. 15260
Copyright © 1992, Jane McCafferty
Manufactured in the United States of America
Printed on acid-free paper

Library of Congress Cataloging-in-Publication Data

McCafferty, Jane.
    Director of the world and other stories / Jane McCafferty.
        p.   cm.
        Contents: World upon her shoulder—The Shadders go away—Help, I'm
    being kidnapped—Eyes of others—While mother was gone with 571—Thirst—
    By the light of friendship—Director of the world—Good-bye now—Replace-
    ment—An evocation.
    ISBN 0-8229-3729-8 (cl)
    I. Title.
PS3563.C33377D57   1992
813'.54—dc20   92-50198
                                                                              CIP

A CIP catalogue record for this book is available from the British Library.
Eurospan, London

"World Upon Her Shoulder" originally appeared in *Mademoiselle;* "The Shadders Go
Away" and "While Mother Was Gone with 571" were first published in the *New England
Review and Bread Loaf Quarterly;* "Eyes of Others" is reprinted from *Writing: Translation of
Memory;* "Thirst" first appeared in *West Branch;* "Director of the World" was originally
published in *Alaska Quarterly Review;* "Replacement" originally appeared in *The Writing
Room: Keys to the Craft of Fiction and Poetry;* and "An Evocation" was first published in *The
Seattle Review.*

The author would like to thank Bernard Kaplan for encouragement given when it was
most needed.

➤ *For Dan*

"Two prisoners whose cells adjoin communicate with each other by knocking on the wall. The wall is the thing which separates them but it is also their means of communication. It is the same with us and God. Every separation is a link."
—Simone Weil

Contents

Director of the World and Other Stories

World Upon Her Shoulder

....

➤ A seven-inch Virgin Mary was glued to the white dashboard of the '67 aqua Nova and usually surrounded by crumpled sheets of lipsticked Kleenex. She stood in all her blue plastic glory throughout the days of my childhood, cheap, constant, and watching the road—unlike the driver, my mother. My mother smelled like Tempest perfume and chain-smoked True Blues. She blamed her great speed and recklessness on the car, which she called Aqua Nova as if it were the car's christened name.

"Come on Aqua Nova," she'd say. "We gotta slow *down!*" Then her foot in her pointy red shoe would slam the gas pedal to the floor and she'd look at me, her shoulders rising up in slow motion to where they'd touch her dangling earrings, her close-lipped mouth stretching out and turning down—gestures that married to mean: What's a person supposed to do when they're stuck with a car like Aqua Nova?

Songs spurted out of the fuzzy AM radio, always turned up too loud. Songs like "Hey Jude" that would cause tears to roll down my mother's face, and she'd turn away from the road, toward me, where I sat color-coordinated in my freshly ironed white dress dabbled with aqua quarter moons; a watchful, skinny child, heavy with a gut-level knowledge that everyone and her mother in this world was doomed.

3

"Rosie," she'd say (one of her many nicknames for me—there was never a reason for any of them, as far as I could tell), "There's nothing like riding around with you and Aqua Nova, hearing a true killer of a song." And if tears ran down her face when she said this, I could see they were tears of fierce joy. Sometimes joy seemed to radiate from every pore on the golden skin that covered her thirty-six year-old-body, and the whole car seemed to fill up with this joy so that it was hard to breathe. Joy like little dabs of bright colors that didn't vanish even when I closed my eyes.

One spring day we were going to the Acme. She had her Carmen Miranda fruit bowl tied with a scarf on top of her head. Carmen Miranda had been a favorite of hers all her life; she'd saved the hat since fifth grade. She had to slump in the seat in order not to bump the fruit on the ceiling. I remember clearly "I Think We're Alone Now" bursting out of the radio, and my mother waited for the part about the beating heart sound, and sang that one line in a quivery, operatic sort of voice, then let whoever it was that sang that song do the rest. She did this to a lot of songs—seized upon one line as if it were the key to something.

We pulled into the Acme parking lot, and she got her usual front-row spot, which is why my father used to call her "Front-Row Hilly." It's a fact that in all the years I rode around with her, she always got the most desirable parking spot. "If you think you'll get it, you'll get it," she said, eyes narrowing.

I knew she was feeling extra good that day because she took my hand and we ran faster than usual toward the store, she in her red flats, I in my brown, round-toed, scuffed and scalloped buckle shoes. We jumped on and off the black rubber mat between the electric eyes and watched the doors flap open and shut, open and shut, until my mother stopped suddenly. She crossed her arms, took a deep breath, put a serious face on under the Carmen Miranda hat, and said, "Shall we enter?"

In the Acme she first said hello to Mrs. Myers, a woman in a flowered housecoat who spent her life sitting on the ledge by the front window—a huge, self-appointed fixture with a taut, red face. "Mrs. Myers," my mother said, "It's so good to see you every week of my life!" and she said this so sincerely that Mrs. Myers's tight, red face stretched into a little smile.

We grabbed a cart and my mother smiled and nodded at each passing shopper. They all smiled back, despite the Carmen Miranda getup. It was as if they knew she wasn't exactly right, but her happiness was too contagious not to catch. Children who rode inside the carts waved to us.

We headed to the aisle where they kept syrup. My mother was saying "Syrup! Exactly! We'll get lots of it!" She began piling bottles of Aunt Jemima into the cart. "Help me do this, will ya?" she said. When we'd filled the entire cart with bottles of Aunt Jemima, she stepped back and said, "OK, now we're talkin'." She took another step back and cocked her head as if to get the proper view. She nodded, biting down on her lower lip.

I'd watched her buy a whole cartful of flesh-colored rubber gloves one time, and the next day she was hauled off to the Delaware State Hospital. I began to make connections and worry.

"You go fetch another cart now, Bird. I think we'll buy a bunch of All," she told me. There was no All in sight, no accounting for her idea. I went to fetch the cart. I moved very slowly and was beginning to feel sick. I stopped by the gum machines and stuck my finger through each silver slot where the gum comes out, then turned and stared out into the parking lot, my heart pounding. There was nothing to do but get the cart and wheel it back to her.

I chose a cart and pushed it, bent down and staring through the spokes. Up ahead I saw her standing by the great mountain of syrup in her cart, grinning wildly. She didn't seem to see me. I grew up considerably in moments like these, digesting my own invisibility.

She pushed the cart of syrup and I pushed the empty one slowly down one aisle and up the next until we got to the detergents. Her face was very solemn now, as if we were suddenly in the heart of a religious ritual.

She wheeled straight to the All and began piling in the boxes. I didn't help this time. I stood looking at my shoes, humming, until the cart was full and she was telling me to follow her to the shortest check-out line. On the way over, a few bottles of syrup cascaded out of my mother's cart. She picked them up and held them in the crook of her arm, then pushed the cart with one hand, controlling it with no problem. This brand of happiness made her strong.

We got in line. People gawked. I smiled at them somewhat apologetically while my mother swayed back and forth as if a great gospel tune were running through her mind. Her smile was so bright it seemed to cut through the glare of the grocery store.

The woman in front of us turned around and said, "Somebody sure loves syrup!" and then smiled, as if waiting for my mother to explain. But my mother just beamed and said she *adored* it, she *worshiped* it, some overblown verb like that, making the woman nod nervously and turn back around quickly. When it came time to ring up the order, the checker gave me a look of sympathy which I pretended not to see.

When we had the Nova packed full with our goods and sat in the front seat ready to go, my mother knocked the side of her head with the heel of her palm and said, "Smokes, Love, I forgot to get smokes. You stay here and I'll be right back."

I sat quietly and watched her fly through the parking lot, then emerge with a carton of True Blues, waving it through the air like a wand. When she got back into the car, she handed me one of two packets of Pep Boys matches. "A Manny, Moe, and Jack for you; a Manny, Moe, and Jack for me," she said. And, rather than remind her that I was not allowed to have matches, that she had told me all my life not to lay a hand on them, I stared at the three men on the cover and slipped the packet into the turtle purse I carried coins and rosary beads in back then.

On the way home, with the back seat full of Aunt Jemima and the trunk packed with All, we sang "Last Train to Clarks-ville"—one of the songs we both had memorized. When it ended, my mother asked if I'd noticed the headline on the *National Enquirer* when we were standing in line back there in the Acme. "No," I said, "Which headline?"

"Man Explodes on Operating Table," she said, then slapped the dashboard next to the Virgin.

"Don't you ever feel like you're on an operating table and you're gonna explode?" she asked me.

"No," I said.

She repeated the headline twice, slapped the dashboard again, and laughed too hard. Then she bit into her forearm so hard she left deep tooth marks. I hung my head out the window like a dog, my eyes squinting in the wind, a prayer in my head, my stringy yellow hair wind-sculpted like a star.

When we pulled up in front of our semidetached, red brick, Wilmington, Delaware, house, Mrs. Tandeminers, the woman who'd been babysitting my infant brother Charlie, came out the front door, eager as usual to help. She carried in the bags, smiling nervously at their contents, not daring to ask why we had bought nothing but syrup and All.

....

In the front hall, as Mrs. Tandeminers was leaving, my mother slapped a twenty-dollar bill into her hand. Mrs. Tandeminers's mouth fell open. She gasped, "No, my word, this isn't right. I've been here just over an hour." And my mother said, "Oh hell, it's the holidays!" and, because it was nowhere near the holidays, Mrs. Tandeminers looked at the floor.

"Look Mrs. Tandeminers. I don't mind paying for quality care and that's what you are with a capital *Q*." My mother opened the door for her and she left, saying, "Thank you, Mrs. Chase, but I really . . ."

My mother closed the door and said it was time to play some records and dance. She began flipping frantically through a stack of 45s on top of the hi-fi, mumbling the titles of songs, half singing them, her knees already dancing. She put on a whole stack of records and then her sister, my Aunt Irene, called on the phone. They talked a while, and I heard my mother saying, "No, I'm fine, damn it. I just happen to be in a *good mood*."

Next thing I knew, we were dancing to the 45s in the living room. My mother, still wearing her hat, danced with Charlie in her arms. He had a faraway, frightened smile on his face. The room was filled with gray light that splashed through the front window.

My Aunt Irene walked in the door. She was obviously there to monitor the mood of my mother. My mother took off her fruit bowl hat and gave it to Aunt Irene to hold on the worn, rose couch. Aunt Irene stared with a nervous grin, watching us dance and hoot. As we danced, the room began to feel lopsided, tilting like a boat, unhitched from the rest of the house and world. I knew Aunt Irene was right to be nervous, but I resented her for this. I was hanging on to a small hope that my mother might be right. What child wouldn't?

"By the way, Irene," my mother said to my aunt in the middle of "The Age of Aquarius."

"By the way what, Hilly?" said my aunt.

"I'm finally gonna sue Jackson's ass and sue it good."

My aunt nodded in fear. It was just as she'd suspected. The obsession was back.

That evening in the dusk-lit kitchen I fed Charlie his baby food. My father walked in, home from work, and I watched him take in all the Aunt Jemimas perched all over the kitchen. I saw him wince, then freeze when he heard my mother upstairs singing a song she had learned in Our Lady of the Seven Sorrows grammar school and had never managed to forget. *Let the mountains skip with gladness!*

My Aunt Irene rushed down from upstairs. "Bobby," she said.

My father looked at my aunt, waiting.

"She just told me she saw the sun spin and she thinks this means she's Saint Bernadette reincarnated. And she wants to sue Jackson again and give all the money to—"

"I'm calling Finch," my father said, rubbing the crease between his eyes. Finch was my mother's doctor. My father looked down at Charlie, who banged on his high chair and said something indecipherable.

When my father called him and reported the syrup and the spinning sun, Finch suggested it was time to go back to Delaware State. Then my father called the cops, knowing from too much previous experience that my mother would refuse to get in the car with him. But she listened to cops. My father told them to come in a few hours, maybe hoping that by that time she would've settled down.

He lifted Charlie up out of his high chair and headed upstairs. I followed behind them and Aunt Irene, who turned around and gave me an irritating, fretful smile midway up.

My mother met us in the hall. She looked beautiful and frightening in a swishing red dress and began dancing around

....

my father in tight circles, her long palms held up outstretched in front of her shoulders and moving back and forth in a rhythm as regular as windshield wipers. She'd stopped singing her hymns and was now doing the Everly Brothers' "Bye Bye, Love." I stared at her palms as if they could hypnotize me. My father stood holding Charlie in his arms. He kissed Charlie's head and closed his eyes for a moment. I looked up at my mother's face, her blue eyes trapped and shining in the faint light of that narrow upstairs hall. She sang right to my father, as if he were someone singled out in a nightclub audience. He opened his eyes and closed them again. Charlie stared at her as my father turned and carried him down the hall and into our bedroom, saying "Jesus Christ."

Soon after, I was in a nightgown and a hooded sweatshirt on the front stoop in the May evening, some light lingering, the slice of sky between the Learys's and Kovaleskis's houses across the street deeply scarlet and blue. The smell of cut grass made the air seem grippable. My mother sat on the stoop beside me. Gathered around us were a few Leary kids, Louis Magee, who was enormous and carried a white mouse with him everywhere, and Piffer Mann, who adored my mother and who was called Piffer the Homo by other boys because he had a high, sweet voice and little enthusiasm for sports. Other kids were in the street popping wheelies on their spider bikes and cussing.

My mother told us how she'd seen the sun spin at four in the afternoon that day, the same as Saint Bernadette centuries before her. Her index finger went around in frantic circles to suggest just how fast the sun did spin. My mother said God was working through her, working through everyone, and all we had to do was listen and realize our missions. She said she would place jukeboxes on the corner of every street, install sliding boards from second story bedroom windows. "You'll get out of bed and climb out the window and slide down to earth." She'd open a huge kitchen for the hungry, serve gourmet food by candlelight. She'd install a swimming pool with underwater music. In the off-season when the pool was drained of water, it could be a merciful place furnished with cots for community napping.

Piffer, going on eleven and smart, pointed out that there was no room left in the neighborhood. Where would she put the pool if all the land was covered by houses and stores?

My mother seemed not to hear the question. "Of course, I'll have the money to do all of this as soon as I sue Jackson," she told us. "And none of you will need to worry about membership dues. I'll be taking care of everything." She winked twice and made a loud clicking sound out of the corner of her mouth.

I watched Piffer's eyes, dark and wide, brimming as usual with intelligent apprehension. I turned to the bright, lopsided moon, rising now in a darkening sky, and watched it shine as my mother began to speak. I had heard her speak this way before, but not in front of all these people.

"Life is transient, children; events are crucial because they are fleeting, encumbered yet empowered by the ephemeral nature of time itself. Sorrow like a hungry demon lurks in every joy; shoes are needed to complete every outfit. We can agree on this much?"

I watched most of her listeners nod.

"Fourteen years ago I was vice-president of the Young Delmarva Catholics for a Better Society society, and we were holding our annual dance, an affair that attracted thousands. The music was provided by the actual Drifters. It was held in the Gold Ballroom of the Hotel Dupont; you can see that I would desire in a pair of shoes some simple eloquence and some clicking sound from the heels. Of course they would need to match my pale green organdy dress with the dark green velvet sash.

I looked from the moon to the faces of the neighbor children and back again. Some of them were beginning to look vaguely frightened or confused. I moved over and sat closer to my mother. I wanted to tell everyone that they could go on home now, go sit on their own front stoop, but I felt somehow my voice was buried too deep inside of me, that if I tried speaking no sound would emerge.

"One day I put myself on the 27D bus and traveled ten minutes down Market Street until we reached Jackson's Exquisite Footwear, where the rich people shopped. I had my savings from the J. Roy Leather Factory in my Atlantic City change purse, sent to me by my father who left us years before for a woman who called herself Hi-C. Like the fruit juice, children, like the fruit juice. In Jackson's, I fell in love with the most becoming and expensive pair of black spike heels I'd ever seen in my life. I tried them on and walked through the store; yes, yes, they made a nice sound, a wonderful sound, and Jackson said, 'Buy them they're gorgeous, and they suit you.'

"I put myself back on the 27D and headed home to Thirty-seventh Street, where I tried the shoes on with my dress, the scoop-neck dress that bristled as if it were living, and that evening I walked up and down the front path while my mother sat on the stoop judging me until the third time up the path when the heel on the left shoe broke off, and I twisted my ankle slightly.

" 'You haul yourself back to that store and tell that man you demand another pair of shoes,' my mother told me." My mother had thoroughly altered her voice to sound like my grandmother, a husky chain-smoker.

"The next day I took the shoes back to Mr. Jackson, who first looked annoyed to see me and then said not to worry, the problem was a minor one and could be remedied with shoe glue.

"'How do you know it won't just break off again?' I said to him.

"He slapped the glue onto the broken heel and stuck it to the shoes, saying 'Trust me, trust me.' I said I just hoped it wouldn't break off at the dance. And then he smiled at me, a smile for which I have no words, a smile containing reproach, and a ravening, roaring presumptuousness, avenging with the greed of thine enemies. I said that if the heel broke off, I'd sue him.

"'Who'd listen to you? You couldn't sue me! You little nobody!'

"He began trying to back me out of the store, while under his tongue were the destructive and flourishing cities of Fraud, Deceit, and Vanity. . . . "

Mrs. Leary came out on her stoop and clapped for the Leary kids to come in for the night. Kate Leary pleaded as usual for my mother to negotiate five more minutes out of her mother.

"I'm telling the kids a little story, Helen," my mother called across the darkening street. "Can they stay five more minutes?"

"Five and five only," came the exhausted voice of Mrs. Leary. As she disappeared back into her house it struck me, as it had many times before, that a neighborhood was a place of separate little worlds—houses that just happened to have ended up facing each other. My mother continued. I saw Kate Leary and her friend exchange looks in the moonlight and understood now that they were laughing at my mother.

"So the night of the dance came. I got myself dressed and my mother stood me in front of the full-length mirror, saying I looked almost as good as Hedy Lamarr in *Her Highness and the Busboy*. Corky Reynolds picked me up in his father's black Ford. The moonlight filled the car and lighted up Corky in his tuxedo as we drove. It was not boring!

"But when we walked into the Gold Ballroom, yes, the heel broke off in the foyer."

My mother spoke at rapid-fire speed, overenunciating every word.

" 'Smoke Gets in Your Eyes' was playing, and Corky shot me a look that said, 'Why'd you get such cheap-o shoes?' I tiptoed on one stockinged foot and one shoe into the dance, holding the broken shoe the way a normal date might hold a clutch purse. When we got to our table I kicked off the other shoe and danced dragging the green organdy on the floor, saying 'It's nothing' each time someone stepped on it.

"Since I'm the sort who likes everything to be *just right*, my evening was spoiled. All I could think of was taking Jackson to court and how with the money I'd put shrubbery in my mother's yard, send her on a cruise ship, buy her decent clothes and seven or eight hats—God that woman looked good in a hat. I pictured a white plush milk-pail hat, an organza turban, a half-hat of royal blue linen deftly swirled with petunia satin and midnight cherries. And she would stop staring out the window each night as if my father was bound to come strolling up the front path, as if she thought she might be able to look hard enough to see him coming back to her—if only she didn't give up the hope, if only she was *religious* about her waiting, yes, then one night he'd simply materialize, and they'd go for a drive with the windows down. . . ."

Mrs. Leary came out and said, "No ifs, ands, or buts," and the Learys left, walking backwards slowly, saying "Bye! Bye! Bye!" all the way to their front door, as was the custom.

By the time the cops arrived at our house that night my mother was making long- and short-distance phone calls to everyone she'd ever loved, liked, or tolerated, even a nun known as the Martin Bomber who had thrown her down the steps in seventh grade. "Remember me, Sister? I ended up married to Bobby Chase, the kid who drove the janitor's car into the rectory wall?" I spied, sitting on the stairs, holding to the white spokes of the banister. I remember little of what she said to anyone else; I knew she would be gone soon, and all I could feel was afraid.

She hung up the phone and shouted the Baltimore Catechism. "Who is God? God is the Supreme Being! Why did God make you? To know Him, serve Him, and love Him in this life and be happy with Him in the next."

Then she walked into the living room and said before a mirror, "Who is God? God's old milk in a black cat cup. Why did God make you? How the hell should I know." Then she did a little tap dance around the room.

When the cops came I went to the doorway of the kitchen where my mother was standing in the corner. The cops were huge in blue uniforms, their shoes gleaming. My mother knew where she was going. I watched her fling open a kitchen cabinet and hunt down a pack of cigarettes. Everyone stared at her as she opened the pack, knocked out a smoke, and lit up. Tears began to stream down her face. She was smiling. "I am so happy," she announced, and exhaled the smoke. "*So happy,*" she repeated.

"Honey, they'll just do a few tests and give you something to make you feel like yourself again," my father told her, gently.

"I don't know how I could possibly feel better than I feel now!" she cried. "I'm happy as humanly possible! I want valentine hearts on my hospital sheets. And I'll be helping the maids again. I will shew forth and perish."

The embarrassed cops escorted her down the hall and out the side door as she continued talking. I ran and followed them out the door. My father called me back and held me still on the stoop. We watched her get into the back seat, still talking. In

the interior car light I saw her turn to look at us before the cop
shut the door.

Days later I visited her in her fifth-floor room. In her
high bed, under a white sheet, in a white gown, she sat up,
flooded in sunlight, drugged. She squinted at me as I walked
toward her.

A strange woman in the next bed said, "Hello there!" as if I
were *her* visitor.

I went and stood at the foot of my mother's bed.

"Sit down," she said.

I sat on the end of the bed and looked down at my hands in
my lap. When I tried to look over at her, the dark circles under
her eyes seemed to throw my glances back to me.

"Maureen Leary fell off her bike and had to have thirteen
stitches in her leg," I finally said.

"She did? Maureen Leary?" my mother said.

"Yeah."

"Hello!" said the woman in the next bed.

"We got a new kid in school," I said.

"Is that right?" my mother said. Her eyes were blue clouds.

"He's been to Japan," I added.

"Japan," she said. "Gosh."

"Hello hello!" said the woman in the next bed, loud and
parrotlike. I would not look up. I could feel her eyes on me like
hands.

From the corner of my eye I saw my mother reach over to
the table and pick up a pack of cigarettes, some strange brand
I'd never seen before. She opened them slowly, taking an un-
usual amount of time just to remove the cellophane. I watched
her face as she chose one from the pack with the utmost care,
as if they weren't all the same. She held the cigarette in front of
her eyes like it was an artifact she couldn't identify. Then she
put the unlighted cigarette in her mouth and sucked on it and

pretended to exhale smoke. "Some nurse gave me this pack. But no matches. Not allowed to have matches. No sir." She sucked harder on the cigarette as if it might spontaneously combust. "They think you'll set yourself on fire," she added.

I unzipped the turtle purse and dug my hand in and held the Pep Boys matches she'd given me days before. A long minute passed, and then I told her I had matches and walked to the side of the bed to stand by her.

I wanted her to tell me to put the matches down, or to hand them over at once, but she looked at me wide-eyed, like a grateful child. I chose a match and struck it, shocked at how easily it lighted. I would be free to light hundreds of them from now on if I wanted. I held the flame next to her cigarette. I watched the tip begin to glow and felt something in me stretch too fast, as if I were the orange ember, lengthening as she inhaled.

The Shadders Go Away

....

> Home from work, she climbed the iron steps that shot up
the back of the pale blue apartment building. The dusk was
bruise colored, winter quick in its lowering down; it always got
dark too early. As she rose past the lit windows of other apart-
ments, she did not look into the small kitchens and bedrooms
that usually drew her eye, but the old man on the fourth floor,
seated by his window as usual, knocked on the dark pane as
she reached the near landing. She looked over at him as he
yanked the window open; it was his ritual to wait for her
return in the evening. "Hi, Mr. Waldman," she said, and
smiled at him framed there, wrapped as usual in a green
blanket, his hair so white it was like a light for the dark in his
room. Though it was part of her day to listen to a piece of
advice he usually offered, to marvel at his weak breath manag-
ing to cloud the outside air as he spoke, tonight she only felt
impatient as he told her, "Foodland's got sliced turkey on sale
today, you oughta get over there."

"Thanks, maybe I will," she said, and resumed climbing.
"I'm in a hurry tonight, I'll talk to you later, OK?"

"The younger boy says you're off for a week in Florida," he
hollered. "Must be nice!"

"We'll bring you something," she called down.

And now she banged on the white door of her apartment,
looking in through the curtains at the empty kitchen, then up

....

at a bright star. "Hey, your wonderful mother's home, and I'm freezing! Let me in!"

Kevin finally swung the door open.

"Hi, Ma," he said, smiling up at her, his eyes almost black and full of their usual clarity, his mouth full and relaxed, his feet in worn boondockers looking rooted to the faded red linoleum; this was ten-year-old beauty entirely supported by grace, so at home was he in his bones and in this world.

"Got a hundred on my history," he told her.

"Did you? You're a genius," she said, picking up the boring stack of mail on the table.

"What time we leavin' tomorrow?" he asked.

"Early. Maybe before the sun comes up. Where's your brother?"

Before he could answer, she heard the TV sizzle into the silence of the den. She set the mail down and walked to the doorway. Leif was crouched before the TV in an old sleeveless undershirt his father had left behind. His shoulder blades stuck out on his wiry back like burdensome wings.

"Hey Leif!" she said. "Excited?" He mumbled "hi" and changed the channels, racing past each station so quickly it was impossible to see what he was dismissing. "Leif, please slow down or you'll break it."

He settled on the evening news, stood up, and backed himself into the blue armchair. She walked over and sat down on the chair across from him and saw he was looking at the news as if it were an opponent he was sure of beating. He cocked up a dark eyebrow, smirked, and then, suddenly, all expression vanished from his face.

"So did you have a good day?" she asked, and imagined that her voice sounded false, excessively cheerful.

"Termites build fortresses sometimes over thirty feet high," he said, and a nervous twitch caused his left eye to wink shut. She felt a sudden urge to cut his hair; it stuck out wildly in every direction, overwhelming his narrow face, accentuating its pale, private look. His sense of privacy made him seem older than twelve sometimes. Something had always been old about him. He'd been one of those wise-looking infants who peered at people when they'd cooed and tickled him.

"Termites live in fortresses?" she said, looking at his profile. He was a big fan of the world's innumerable creatures lately, absorbing facts he heard on nature programs like he absorbed everything else. He recited the facts as if they fit naturally into any conversation. How could you tell a boy like Leif that some things were off the subject? Did there have to be a subject? She looked at his large hands, stretched out on the arms of the blue chair like starfish. He was listening to the news so intently it seemed he was unaware that she was in the room.

Back in the kitchen, at the black table by the window, she looked out at the moon. On the table sat a globe bank full of money they'd saved for gas to get them to Florida. Her hand reached out and gave it a spin, and the cascade of coins was the sound of hope falling through the small, knowable world.

Kevin came in from outside, coatless, his face red with cold.

"Where'd ya go?" she asked him.

"Nowhere. Just seein' what it was like out," he said. "Can I make popcorn to celebrate Florida and all?"

"Good idea."

In the bedroom she turned on a lamp, undressed, wrapped herself in a flannel robe, and stood at the dresser mirror brushing her hair. Some night when the boys were sleeping after a day of swimming and sun, she'd sit at the bar of the hotel, tan in a new sundress, writing a postcard, drinking an exotic drink, and someone would come sit beside her and—she stopped herself, as if even in fantasy you could spoil things by expecting too much. Now she saw herself and the boys driving the next day in the old Comet until they reached warmth—some solid state like North Carolina. They'd stop at a restaurant, and she'd

....

surprise them saying, Get anything you want. They'd talk about perfectly average things that would all sound new being uttered into the air of a strange place.

She put the brush down, and her green eyes collided with their reflection in the mirror. A clear image of the three of them in some restaurant suddenly sent her spirit sinking. Her husband had been at his best in restaurants—making the waitress laugh, telling the kids stories, ordering elaborate desserts no matter how broke they were. "They're in New Mexico making a life for themselves," she said aloud now, as she often did, like a person explaining it to another person who was slow. *Themselves* was the word that hurt. Sometimes at night, startled awake by the space beside her where he'd always been, she'd say the word as if it could push her to the depths of her loss, to the edge of it. As if such limits existed.

They shared the popcorn while a squid took up the entire TV screen.

"Squids use jet propulsion," Leif said. "They can get away from *anything.*"

"Mmmmm," she said, but Kevin just sighed dramatically.

"Is there a problem?" she asked Kevin, and watched his dark head fall back on the gray couch into a circle of lamplight.

"Leif acts mental," he whined, as if his brother were not present. Leif looked over at Kevin, then back at the squid, as if they were equally phenomenal.

"Don't say that. Don't say 'mental.' I *hate* that." But part of her resented Leif's excessive concentration, his widened eyes so intensely focused on the squid—a monstrous, mottled urchin, its tentacles long and slithery and groping at nothing.

"Cute little thing, isn't it?" she said, and grabbed some popcorn.

The narrator of the program was now saying what Leif had

already told them about jet propulsion, and Leif nodded in agreement like a teacher with a promising student.

"Mom, I have to watch Miss America tonight because Eddie Padaclaro's sister is Miss Pennsylvania and all these kids made bets and stuff."

"And did Kevin Shadder make a bet?" She knew he had. He was always betting on something.

"Sort of," he said. She stared at him, waiting.

"I sort of put twenty packs of hockey cards on Miss North Dakota," he confessed.

"Twenty packs!" she said, and now he, too, stared with great interest at the squid.

"Who the hell is Miss North Dakota?"

He shrugged. She was about to say something about the value of money and caught herself. This was the night before the trip, and therefore a part of the trip, and she wanted things to be perfect. She put her arm around Kevin and pulled him close.

"I'll give ya Miss North Dakota," she told him, laughing.

"If you count the tentacles, you'll see this is your average squid," Leif assured them, one of his long legs beginning to bounce up and down, as if all the reckless energy in his body had suddenly gathered there.

After "Life on Earth" ended, Leif said goodnight and walked back to his room, and she and Kevin stayed up to watch the pageant. She fixed them each a cup of hot chocolate, but fell asleep before she had a chance to drink hers. She woke up to Kevin shouting, "Hi Anita!" as if Eddie Padaclaro's sister, Miss Pennsylvania, could hear him as she smiled into the camera and told America she was interested in finance and children.

"I'm hittin' the sack," she finally told Kevin. "Don't be up too late." He was too immersed in the pageant to say much of a goodnight. His interest surprised her. She fell asleep pretending her bed was a raft in the middle of the gulf, the faces of her sons emerging from the water, moonlit and calm.

"Birds don't fly unless they have to," Leif said at the kitchen table the next morning, his face blurred and distant with sleep. The kitchen was chilly in the light of dawn; Kevin had the hood of his red sweatshirt pulled up and tied tightly under his chin. They were eating French toast, everyone's favorite.

"I've heard that," she said. "It's interesting."

"If they get enough water and food they stay right where they are and forget how to fly. Their bodies forget. Like the penguin when—"

"This is the best French toast I ever had!" Kevin shouted, his black eyes shooting over to Leif, then down at his plate.

"Do you need to shout?"

She watched Leif cut into his toast and knew he'd dropped the subject of birds, knew behind his lowered eyes the first nameable sadness of his day was forming.

"Maybe we'll see dolphins in Florida," she said. "Leif, what do you know about dolphins?" Lief shrugged while Kevin did a bad imitation of a noisy dolphin.

"I really hope we see some," she said, and her eyes fell on Leif's long-fingered hands. Holding the silverware in this light, they looked beautiful and certain. Kevin tried again to imitate a dolphin and nearly choked on his food. She hit him on his back until he coughed up a piece of breakfast, his face bright red and his eyes wet with fright, staring at her as if he might cry. And then he smiled.

She carried a battered brown suitcase down the back steps, and Kevin opened the trunk of the Comet. The sound of the trunk slamming shut said, *this is your trip. Begin.*

Now that they were leaving, the excitement that had been so pure when she'd imagined this moment was laced with anxiety, and a sudden fear spread through her, dark and palpable as the bare catalpa branches that spread into the red sky across the street. She looked at the side of the blue apartment building and for a moment wanted to cancel everything. It struck her as a place that might crumble or ascend as soon as you turned your back on it.

But they got into the car, Kevin in the back with a cassette player, Leif in the front with a book. As they backed onto the street, Kevin's tape player blared, shredding the morning silence.

"I don't think so, Kevin," she said.

"Fall, fall baby, fall down on me!" shouted the singer before he was quieted.

They hit the freeway where trucks roared by at top speed, dwarfing them, the drivers staring down as they passed. Blond reeds in the glistening marsh to their left arched back in the wind while the sun rose up ahead of them on the right, caught between a billboard and a tower storing water? Gas? Poison? It was a deep red sun bleeding in a sky now turning a generous blue, and she was electrified by the coming light, the clarity of the bitter air.

"We're flyin'!" Kevin said from the backseat. He was upside down now, his head hanging off the edge of the seat, his feet in green hightops on the back ledge, jiggling. Leif sat in the passenger seat, his finger tracing lines on a map of the South.

"There's a llama farm in Virginia," Leif said, looking over at her. "We should take a detour and see it."

"Oh honey, I don't think so," she said. "Not today." Leif went back to his map, and Kevin put on one of his father's old tapes: John Hartford singing "Gentle on My Mind."

"Llamas are shy as shit," Leif said.

"Leif, you watch that talk," she said, and began to sing along with the tape, determined not to think of anything the song might recall. She drove, aware of her own hands on the wheel,

the silver van in front of them with the bumper sticker reading
Take Back the Night, the woods flying by on either side of them,
the sun hidden now behind clouds that thickened as they entered the state of Delaware.

It began to snow lightly, and Leif put his hand up to the
windshield where the flakes landed, as if their crystalline perfection might leak through the pane and into his palm. Seeing
this gesture of his filled her with the desire to do something
nice for him, maybe change her mind about the llamas. She
imagined Leif amazed in a field surrounded by white and
brown llamas. Didn't llamas have a habit of spitting at people?
She could see him being spit at in the face. It would happen to
him. No detours.

The snow fell more heavily, and she turned on the windshield wipers. Kevin swayed back and forth in the backseat,
imitating them.

"I'm the human windshield wiper!" he said. Leif turned
around to look at him.

"Calm down, Kev," she said.

"I gotta pee," Leif said.

She told him a rest stop would be coming up soon, but a mile
later he demanded she pull over to the side of the road. He
hopped out and ran up a grassy embankment. Rather than
turning his back, he turned to the side. She bowed her head
and rubbed her eyes.

"Leif!" Kevin said, as if his brother could hear him. She
looked back at Leif. Behind the quick lines of snow that shot
through the gray air like bars, he stood zipping up his pants, his
face squinting and turned to the side. The tall sky behind him
rose up darkly, tight as a wall. He looked very small standing in
front of it. He walked toward the car, shoulders hunched
against the cold, hands in the pockets of his black corduroy
coat that she saw now was too small for him.

"Hope ya know the whole entire highway saw your jewels,"

Kevin told him as she started up the car. Leif was looking at the map once again.

"Next time you could at least turn your back," she said. "It wouldn't hurt. I mean, really, Leif."

She drove, taking comfort in the number of cars flanking their own, all of them moving in the same sure direction through the same thick light, into the city of Baltimore where the snow began to ease up, where old train yards, abandoned factories, and glaring billboards against the dreary sky all joined to make her happy just to be passing through. They passed a car graveyard that went on for a mile—flattened, rusted cars torn and stacked like jagged mountains; Leif hung his head out the window to see, and she let him. Kevin sang an old song he'd been singing for weeks. His voice was childish, almost babyish, and sometimes he'd grow self-conscious and suddenly drop a few octaves.

Wild horses
Couldn't drag me away
Wild, wild horses . . .

"Kevin, sing something else."

A sense of weariness came over her and deepened for a moment when she looked at her hands on the steering wheel, chapped from cold, the veins showing. She'd get lotion in Florida. She'd get smooth and dark all over.

Wild, wild horses
We'll ride them someday.

On the outskirts of Baltimore they stopped at an Arco and each bought a can of Coke while a heavy man with a naked woman tattooed on his arm put some gas in the Comet.

They drove and drove, all three of them quiet, seemingly hypnotized by the speed, the bare trees that lined the freeway now, the engine's hum, the fact that the road kept going. They drove all day, straight into evening light and the warmth she'd been waiting for. All the windows were rolled down and the late light whipped through the car and rushed through their hair and up their shirtsleeves.

"I'm starved," Kevin whined.

"I know, pretty soon we stop," she promised, and a while later pulled into the parking lot of a South Carolina 7-Eleven. The sudden lack of motion made their bodies heavy, and silence for a moment seemed to pin them in place. Then they all got out, stretched, groaned, and went in for burritos. She didn't want to waste time in a restaurant. She just wanted to *be there.* She was exhausted.

In the car they ate their burritos and she sipped on a huge cup of coffee. They stared bleary-eyed into the 7-Eleven, watching the customers stand in line as if the storefront were a drive-in movie screen. Every minute or so someone would exit, purchase in hand. An old woman came out and accidentally dropped her Slurpee onto the cement near the door; she looked down at the emerging red slush as if it had nothing to do with her, then walked away.

"Can I go get that and drink what didn't spill?" Kevin asked.

"Just sit still."

They stared ahead, eating in silence. Finally Leif said, " 'Member that time Dad bought us fireworks and that old dog went nuts when we lit 'em?"

"They weren't fire*works,* they were fire*crackers,*" Kevin said. She started up the car.

Kevin curled up in the backseat and fell asleep while Leif stayed wide awake, his green eyes fixed on the low stars ahead. Cars occasionally whizzed by on either side of them, streaking their faces with light. She looked over at Leif's lit profile and was struck as she often was at how similar it was to her own.

"You could never deny that one's yours," people said, even when he'd been a baby.

She turned on the radio and found a song she liked, a song

that for a moment blasted her back so that she was young, a new mother in a city park.

"Leif, when this song was big I was pushing you in a stroller. You wore a little blue cap. I can see you clear as day in that sunny park. You loved it."

"Cincinnati," he said.

"Right. Everywhere you went you had to wear that blue cap."

She smiled over at him; he was looking out the window.

Miles later, he spoke up to inform her that the baleen whale was four times larger than the largest known dinosaur. "Nobody thinks about that, just because it's in the ocean." She had an urge to say, "So what." She felt her foot put pressure on the gas, like a reflex, as if she could drive away from this fact, drive away from all the facts he offered up lately as if he had nothing else to give.

"Oh Leif," she sighed. "You know a lot of things, don't you?"

He waited for a few seconds before he said, in a voice so even it was eerie, "I know more than you think."

She laughed nervously, looking at him, headlights splashing over him, then leaving him dark again.

"I know a lot of things and personally hate everything," he said on top of her laughter. Her palms tightened on the wheel as her laughter left her.

"If some idiot dropped some nuclear bombs on us, I'd think it was funny. I really would," he said. He leaned out the window and spit.

"Leif, come on now, what are you talking about?"

"I'd think it was a good idea," he said, then laughed suddenly. It was a laugh of disgust with a cry in its center, a laugh too deep, too old to come out of the mouth of a twelve-year-old boy; the laugh echoed inside of her, and she felt suddenly that he was a complete stranger, and though she wanted to she could not look over at him. She turned the radio up.

....

"I can't stand oldies anymore," she said, then pretended to be utterly absorbed in finding a good station.

"Static drives me crazy; I'd rather listen to bad songs clearly than good ones through static, ya know?" The air gushing into the car smelled sweet now, a full, dark wildflower smell that vanished as soon as she tried to breathe it in. She found a song she liked and attempted to sing along, but the sound of her own voice filled her with enormous sadness, a sadness that was new and foreign because of its size, its heaviness. Was it even sadness at all? Was it fear? She tried singing again, but the feeling deepened, widened. It was fear; was it fear? She sat up very straight and tried to smile and felt Leif looking over at her. His voice began explaining something, something about whales, about whales singing, how water transmits sound better than air, how whales can hear each other over thirty miles away.

"Leif?" she said, her voice wavering. She couldn't think of what else to say. She glanced over her shoulder at Kevin, a small boy in the back, curled up alone.

"Kevin's asleep," she said, as if that were relevant and interesting.

"I think we should stop at a rest stop soon," she said, but now the sound of her own voice terrified her; it seemed the only real thing in or outside the car.

I'm caving in, she thought.

"Who?" she heard herself say.

An image of her husband came into her mind—as he had looked coming up the steps one day with a package in his arms. She saw his dark eyes now and felt nothing, no sorrow, no rage, only this caving in that was happening both quickly and slowly. Then the steps were empty. She tried to think of somebody else, anybody who she might be driving toward, a person, a human being who could take her hand and say *Lydia Shadder* and stop this feeling, the terror of this caving in.

"We're going to Florida," she said. "Florida." She laughed; the whole idea of thinking you could drive somewhere to get away! She looked out her side window at the sky. It seemed so much smaller than what she had inside of her; it seemed pathetic, its bright stars cheap scattered trinkets, its dark expanse something she could swallow in a glance, and inside of her it would be lost. Another laugh escaped her.

Leif suddenly leaned out his window and shouted into the air that rushed toward him, sending his words back like paper scraps.

"I hate this state! This whole state of South Suck Me Carolina! And all the other goddamned states!"

"Leif," she shouted. Was it a shout? Had she only whispered?

"Mom?" came the fearful, sleepy cry of Kevin from the back.

"Fuck!" Leif screamed at a small yellow car now keeping pace beside them. "Fuck you!"

She felt herself reach over and yank hard on his shirt, and he leaned farther out the window and pounded the side of the Comet.

"Get him in here!" she cried. "Bring him back in here!"

Kevin leaned over the seat and yanked on Leif's collar and hammered violently on his back. When Leif started to come in, Kevin flung himself backwards, crying.

Leif sat with his hands over his face, one leg moving back and forth. She would continue to drive. It was a simple thing, driving, and they were going to Florida.

"Mom!" Kevin cried. "What's wrong?"

"Everyone in the world will now shut up," Leif said from behind his hands, and then his hands left his face and clapped over his ears, elbows jutting out on either side.

"Shut up, shut up, shut up," he said, and continued. It was as if he planned to sit and say those words forever, as if he'd chosen this chant knowing she'd have no choice but to join him when she turned from the road to demand he shut up.

"We could find a place to stop," she said, keeping her eyes on the Comet's headlights, two bright beams tunneling into the dark, small and parallel.

Help, I'm Being Kidnapped

➤ Horace was a famous photographer and the middle-aged boyfriend of Rosa. Rosa was the woman who tried to teach me to play the violin one year in southern New Jersey. I'll tell you about Horace after I tell you some other things.

Rosa's hair rippled down to her ankles. She wore peasant dresses back then and wire-frame glasses, and her southern-belle voice (she was a transplant from Macon, Georgia) was childish, though she must have been at least thirty. I was thirteen, about to turn fourteen at the time, and I'd signed up to take violin lessons from her after I'd heard her play at a fair, barefoot in red autumn leaves. I had never wanted to play violin before that; I'd never heard classical music in my life. My parents belonged to a record club, but mainly they sent away for people like Glen Campbell. I'd grown up on music that some people might say was so bad it was good. For instance, I knew all the words to Bobby Goldsboro's "Honey" when I was six years old. ("She was always young at heart / Kind of dumb and kind of smart.") You might not know that song, but you can take my word for it, it's only one or two leagues above Paul Anka's "Havin' My Baby," which you might not know either, in which case you'll just have to trust me when I say I'd been exposed to much schlock, along with some good stuff like

33

....

Johnny Cash Live at San Quentin. My father liked to sit and drink and cry for the prisoners.

But at that age I had taste quite different from my parents, of course. I liked to croon that old song, "Helpless, helpless, helpless," in the nasal whine of Neil Young. "What's your problem?" my mother would say, "are you retarded?" "Big birds flying across the sky," I'd sing for an answer. "Throwing shadows on our eyes."

Really, I wanted to take violin lessons from Rosa mainly because she was a hippie, and I wanted to go over to her house and sit in the glass room where she taught and absorb the atmosphere. It was a way to get out of my middle class suburb for a while at a time when I was beginning to understand its limitations. It was a tract suburb—the split-level houses all the same and none of them over twenty years old. Rosa and Horace lived in a place I thought of as a village, in a house I privately called *a bungalow*, then later, when I learned more lingo, *a crash pad.*

My lessons were on Saturday afternoons. It often rained on those Saturdays, which increased the mystery of being there. The glass walls were streaked with long, meandering drops of silver, and the huge trees outside were a deeper shade of green. I felt like I was in England for some reason, though I'd never been out of the state of New Jersey, except to Washington, D.C., on a class trip where the hordes of 1970 protestors captivated me more than the monuments. Behind the glass room was another room in which usually two or three artist types would be gathered, talking about books or politics. They had beards and nasal, almost lazy, voices like the deejays on FM stations. Diligent girlfriends had patched their faded bell-bottom jeans. They said the word *real* when they meant good, or happy, or anything positive. These potatoes are *real*. You had to pronounce the word as if you were wearing a nose plug.

After my lesson, to my delight, Rosa would always invite me to sit among them. They were who I thought I wanted to be when I grew up.

But they were men. I didn't want to grow up and be a man, but I did want to be like them, which was a conflict, I knew, but chose to ignore that sort of thing most of the time. It wouldn't have suited me to think of growing up to be like Rosa, who was too quiet and delicate, too passive.

And the few other female hippies I'd been around seemed a lot like Rosa. It was clear to me that the hippie men were the ones who were exciting, smart, and funny. Mostly their girl-friends maintained a certain look and behaved as their appreciative audiences. I'd seen Rosa serve them all lunch more than once, a demure, barefoot waitress, smiling in the steam of the meal she'd prepared.

I liked Rosa and also admired her and sensed the little-girl voice she spoke in was a fake somehow. And I felt betrayed by her on some level, that she didn't speak up loud and clear, that she looked at those men too reverently, as if she wasn't equal to them. I wanted her to step out of her role, I see now, though I couldn't articulate any of that to myself then; I had no idea what a "role" even was.

Of course it wasn't just Rosa who left me feeling somehow betrayed. There was my mother, our neighbors, my aunt. It was the style in that suburb to let a man gently or not so gently push you around, to let them lay down the rules, to spend your spare energy trying not to look like a "frumpy housewife." They all used that word *frumpy* too much. Do I look frumpy? they'd ask each other. No, no! You don't look the least bit frumpy!

I knew I didn't want to turn out like them, even if they did have a lot of good points. Meanwhile, the men I knew—fathers, uncles, neighbors—surely had their own brand of misery, but from my perspective they were mysteries in cars, sliding away to run the world, I thought, winking at me as they rounded the corners where I stood bouncing a ball.

Horace was Rosa's boyfriend and much older—maybe fifteen or twenty years older—and he was the one who saw how fascinated I was with the bohemian shelter they had going. He thought my interest—my awe—was amusing, no doubt, but also, to be fair, Horace had a genuine urge to enlarge my mind and deepen my sensibility, the instinct of all great teachers. So after violin lessons, I'd step out of the rainy glass room and into the livingroom, if you could call that sprawl of pillows and candles and weird antiques a livingroom, and Horace would recommend books and tell me about why they were great, books like *Summerhill* and *Dandelion Wine* and *The Brothers Karamazov* and even *Civilization and Its Discontents*. I felt like I was finally being educated with real ideas; my mind churned as he spoke, and I was always grateful and afraid that I wasn't grasping enough.

One day I showed up for my violin lesson early; Rosa was teaching another student—some tall boy named Arthur Hastings—who played so well I almost decided to quit, imagining that I was the student Rosa dreaded most, imagining she and Horace and the others secretly called me "the Squeaker"—and anyhow, I was out on the back stoop that late spring day under a gray sky listening to Arthur pour himself into what may have been Mozart and feeling like the most inferior creature on earth, the way only a young girl raised on Bobby Goldsboro and Glen Campbell can feel.

Suddenly, Horace opened the green door to his darkroom, which was out back, a little brick room he'd made himself. He stood there framed in the doorway, that tall dashiki-wearing, dark-haired man who liked enlarging minds, and looked at me without speaking. This is important, because it tells you a lot about Horace. That he would stand in a doorway and stare at you like this when you were fourteen. Stare for about a minute while you smiled nervously, gave a little wave, and even murmured, "Hi, Horace." Finally he cleared his throat and stepped out of the doorway and walked toward me, a tall, powerfully built man. He wore new sandals. Silver streaked his thick hair.

"Well, young lady," he said, "what's on your mind today?"

(I cringed inwardly; "young lady" always felt like a kind of insult.)

"Nothing much. How are your pictures turning out?"

"Very well, thanks. Would you like to see some?"

"OK."

He had what I can only describe as burning blue eyes, and yet they were cold. The penetrating eyes of a mind reader. I was supremely uncomfortable with him, yet drawn to that discomfort because it was new and somehow seemed the opposite of boredom.

I followed him into his office, which was built onto the house as an addition. On his wooden desk were huge piles of photographs. He showed me about ten of them. They were all of women. Just dramatic faces. Captivating. I wished that I could be in the room alone so I could look at them without his eyes hovering over me and waiting for my response to each one.

"I wish I was a photographer," I said, and I meant it. I have always wanted to be just about everything.

"So why not work with me," Horace said.

I looked up into his ice blue eyes, but couldn't hold that gaze.

"Really?" I said. "I could work with you?"

"I need a helper. You could be my apprentice. I could teach you how to develop pictures. You could join me on my shoots. I need help carrying my equipment."

"Well, OK, that sounds great to me. Thank you!"

....

My heart pounded in gratitude, along with fear that he'd change his mind. Horace told me to be over at their place starting Saturday at nine in the morning. Then, when school let out, I could start coming every day if I wanted.

I remember the first photograph I saw that Saturday. We were in the darkroom with a small light on in the corner, and Horace called me over to his side. It was a black-and-white photograph of a woman in a cage, a cage suspended from the ceiling. The picture was still wet and clothespinned to a piece of rope. The woman wore next to nothing, and her hair was white-blonde, and her shoes were spiked heels, and underneath the cage a bunch of men were yelling things up to her, their faces contorted while hers was cool, placid, smiling.

"What do you think of this?" Horace said.

"I don't know," I said. I was completely embarrassed.

"This was taken about two miles away from where we stand right now. In a place called Roxy Divine's. Have you ever seen that place?"

"No."

"So what are your impressions of this picture? What do you see?"

"I don't know. Woman in a cage."

Horace sighed and shrugged. We were quiet for a while. Then it was pitch black; he was developing something else.

"Tell me," he said, "do you know why you deny the existence of sexuality?"

I stood a foot away from him, my face beginning to burn. "I don't deny that," I said, but I couldn't even bring myself to say the word *sexuality*. I had a sometimes boyfriend whom I'd French-kissed before quite a few times, drunk on sloe gin in his basement slow dancing to "Nights in White Satin" and "Neither One of Us Wants to Be the First to Say Good-bye," but I didn't want to talk about any of it with this man named Horace.

"Oh yes you do deny it, it's very obvious to me," he said. "The way you dress, the way you hold your body. You're a beautiful girl, but you carry yourself like a boy. And you dress like a boy, too. You hide your figure."

I let the subject drop. In the total blackness of the darkroom, I felt his energy and an odd mixture of embarrassment, resentment, and confused, excruciating eroticism, trapping me.

When summer rolled around, I began working with him four or five times a week. I made it a point to dress more like a boy than ever before, showing up in my brother's oversized New York Giant's football shirt, my hair in a braid, my cut-off shorts down to my knees, and battered, graffitied sneakers on my feet. He would always look me up and down, making no effort to disguise what seemed his baffled disgust. Sometimes he even said something like, "So, Champ, where's the big game?" I think I dressed this way in the same defiant spirit that some women, when they age, decide to flaunt their sagging bodies and wrinkles.

In the darkroom, when it was pitch black, the idea—no, the energy—of sex usually somehow filled the air like invisible fire. In his plastic tray of chemicals, pictures of women (in clothes) were coming to life, while he said things to me like, "Sex rules this world, you know. And the sooner you accept that, the happier you'll be."

I'd say, "It does not rule the world! It's a part of life, but it doesn't rule the world! You only think it rules the world!"

"Methinks the lady doth protest too much," he said. I didn't know where the hell he got that from, but it really irritated me.

He'd flick on the tiny lamp in the corner and call me over to watch the last stage of the women developing in the tray,

....

blurry faces and bodies submerged under liquid, getting clearer in the magic chemical potion. Faces, shoulders, breasts, legs. Exotic clothing.

"What do you think?" he'd always say.

"Nice."

But soon he began to develop pictures of a woman in the nude, as they say. She'd be standing under a tree in one picture, sitting in a black rocking chair in another picture, stretched out on a shag carpet in yet another. She had long, dark hair, a stern, almost offended-looking face, large breasts I tried to avoid, thighs that he told me were voluptuous.

"She doesn't look so happy," I said once. He had printed one particular photograph of this "nude" about ten times; all ten of her hung on the rope, some drying, some still wet. He was trying to decide what print was the best.

"Happy?" he said. "No, she's not happy. I don't know any happy women."

The remark didn't shock me. I said, "What about Rosa?"

"Rosa! You think Rosa's happy?" He laughed.

"I don't know," I said.

"I think you're more perceptive than that," he said.

He had a way of complimenting me that further confused the ambiguous feelings I had for him. He was, after all, a famous photographer—he even had a book published—and he had those mind-piercing blue eyes, which gave his compliments weight; I quickly absorbed them into my shaky identity. Yes, I'd think, I'm very *perceptive*.

"Most intelligent women are unhappy," he said. "In fact, every intelligent woman I know is unhappy in some way."

"Why?"

"Why? Because they're women," he said, and laughed.

I didn't press him on this. I was afraid it would have something to do with sex.

That wasn't the only thing we talked about. I remember he explained to me what "freon" was, for instance, and how it worked in refrigerators. He also told me all about B. F. Skinner. "Sounds like an idiot," I said of him, and Horace threw his head back and laughed. Another time he told me all about the anthropologist Colin Turnbull. "I wouldn't mind being an anthropologist," I said, and Horace laughed and said, "I'm not sure that would be your field. Too sexual."

So, eventually, almost everything somehow meandered back to that topic in the darkroom, as if to prove his theory that sex ruled the world. And he thought nothing of asking me things like, "Do you have a boyfriend? Do you feel desire for him? Or is it platonic?"

I remember the acute embarrassment of hearing my voice in the pitch blackness say, "I feel desire for him." I would never have said that without that cloak of total darkness, and I wasn't even exactly sure it was true. But I was invisible in there. I was a disembodied voice. It was a kind of freedom that I loved and hated at the same time, and I was aware that I was losing something, some self I'd been before I'd taken these verbal risks in the dark.

Meanwhile, I was still taking violin from Rosa, who gave me new, bemused smiles, as if Horace was telling her about our conversations. "Horace thinks you'll make a decent photographer," she said once, smiling. She must have been a little relieved that the Squeaker had another interest.

Horace let me take a bunch of pictures one day at some inner-city fair; he'd been hired by a local arts chapter to try to capture the spirit of the happening, and he felt sure he'd captured it, so he handed the camera to me. I decided I'd photograph only men and boys, sensing that day the power of the camera, the power of being the one who sees and is not seen. When we developed those eight photographs of

....

mine, Horace said, "These are good photographs, but men bore me."

"Not me," I said. I enjoyed clothespinning those wet men to the rope, then stepping back and pretending to figure out which ones I liked best.

Horace was taking me on a shoot again. He had to take a bunch of pictures of jazz musicians who were playing downtown in an open square, but first we had to ride about twenty minutes out of town to a camera shop; he needed special film.

The day was hot and bright. Horace had requested that I not dress like a football player when we went on shoots, so I was in a blouse and short blue skirt, with my hair down and smooth, and red sandals with heels that belonged to my mother. Horace insisted on taking pictures of me that day before we got in the car. I was both flattered and reluctant to join the ranks of his subjects. In those pictures I'm leaning against the outside of the brick darkroom with my arms crossed and my eyes averted. I'm skinny, with long straight hair, and look younger than fourteen. I have something in common with those girls Edvard Munch liked to paint.

We were on the highway driving through the hot white light of afternoon, going fast in his blue car, all the windows down and no radio music playing. We'd had a conversation about something, but nothing that I can really remember. Then a silence fell. It was a heavy silence. I looked down at my legs. They looked too bare, too white, and I felt how sweaty they were against the vinyl seat. I tried stretching my skirt to make it longer; I had a sudden, desperate desire to cover up. I looked at my feet trapped in my mother's red heeled sandals. They also looked too exposed, vulnerable. I'd even carefully painted my toenails bright red that morning in the bathroom, then stood admiring them before the full-length mirror. Looking at them now filled me with intense regret. Horace had noticed them earlier, smiling his approval. I had the polish with me in a small white shoulder bag, and I took it out now and held it tightly in my fist. My heart was pounding, and I wasn't sure why, but I began to feel afraid. The silence continued, and when I stole a look over at Horace, I saw he was lost in his own thoughts, but that was no comfort.

I had a spiral notebook with me. I always brought one to the shoots; I liked to write down the fascinating things I saw. I opened the book to a clean page and unscrewed the white top of the nail polish bottle, and, as if in a dream or a nightmare, I began to paint a message with that polish. The first word was *help*. Horace smelled the polish and looked over at me, and I pretended to be painting my fingernails. "Just painting my nails," I said, my own voice sounding small and alien. He smiled and went back to his thoughts. I darkened the word *help*. Then, without thinking, *I'm being kidnapped* were the next three words I painted, and I watched the hot air dry them almost immediately. I looked down at my sign, then quietly turned to my side window, holding my message up to the world of passing cars. "Help, I'm Being Kidnapped," the red letters screamed, and I watched as the various drivers glanced over, some of them doing double takes, some of them slowing down to read it, and all of them simply driving along, figuring it wasn't any of their business.

But soon enough a driver took my message seriously. Horace was pulling onto a ramp, an exit, and the driver, a man in a green pickup truck with a woman beside him, pulled in front of Horace and turned his truck sideways on the ramp, blocking us. Horace had to slam on the breaks; the tires screeched and he said, "What the fuck is going on here?" as he watched the man from the truck walk toward us. I remember the blanched terror on Horace's face. He looked almost childish. Something in him had collapsed. His own sense of power and control had completely vanished, and this change in him scared me as much as the sight of the man walking toward us. I was seeing too much of Horace, too much of the vulnerability I hadn't even begun to imagine was there in him. He was sweating now, and I was filled with a paralyzing guilt.

The man stood at the window now. He leaned down and said to Horace, "You kidnapping her?" The man smelled powerfully of alcohol. His black hair was greased back except for one fallen clump dividing his forehead.

"What are you talking about, sir?" Horace asked, his terror still evident on his white face.

"I ain't got time for liars," the man said. "Now if you're kidnapping her—"

"He's not," I said, with great urgency. "I'm all right, really I am, it was just a joke."

"A joke? What kind of goddamned joke is that?"

Horace had turned his pale face toward me; I looked at the man, avoiding Horace's eyes.

"Billy?" a woman's voice cried out. I saw she'd gotten out of the truck and was now rushing toward us. By this time a few cars were backed up on the ramp behind us, and one of the drivers was laying on the horn relentlessly. "Billy! Jaysus, what are you talking about?" Now the woman stood next to the man. She was a very tan woman with bleached hair and her eyes made up. She leaned in through the window and looked at me. "Where's your little sign, sweetheart?" she said.

I looked at her as if I didn't know what she meant.

"Your sign," she said, "Your damn cry for help sign!" She was angry now.

I had little choice but to hold it up for all to see. I looked out at the sky, away from all their eyes, as I did this. Horace said, "Good God, this girl's insane! Listen, I'm sorry for the trouble. She's not being kidnapped. There's no problem here. Except maybe a severe mental problem."

"How can we be sure?" the woman said.

"There's no problem. I'm sorry for your trouble," I said.

"Is he making you say this?" the man said. "Because if he is, you give me the nod, and I'll go get my gun and give it to him in the head."

"Billy!" the woman said.

"No, really, he's not a kidnapper. It was all me, mister, it was me. Just a stupid joke! I'm sorry!"

This time they believed me. Both the man and woman shook their heads at us. They got back into their truck and now we sailed down the clear ramp in silence.

"Sorry," I said. My face was red with shame, guilt, and a deep feeling of estrangement from myself, like a big part of me was a bird flying above the car. I had no idea why I'd made that sign, or why all I wanted now was to be alone so I could cry.

"Sorry?" he said. "I could have been killed."

I badly wanted him to regain his rational way of speaking, his control, his poise, his power. But his voice was shaky and his face still had no color. We rode along through the bright summer air in silence.

Finally, he piped up and said in a mocking voice, "Help, I'm being kidnapped!"

Another silence.

"What I want to know," he said, "Is why on earth you did that. Why did you make the sign? What motivated you?"

Now I was somewhat relieved; his eyes were once again penetrating, his control was returning to him slowly but surely.

"I don't know," I said. "I can't explain."

I had my hand out in the wind and took small comfort in that feeling of resistance. He pressed me for a while to try to explain, then gave up.

"I think I understand," he said, and a smile came to his lips, then disappeared. "You have a secret desire somewhere inside of you, a desire for me to take you away, to 'kidnap' you, somehow, don't you?"

"No!"

He smiled at the intensity of my response. Had I not been so consumed with an inexplicable sadness meshed with relief that we'd survived Billy and his gun, I would have wanted to scream at that smile.

"It's nothing to be ashamed of," he said. "I understand now. You acted out of fear. Fear of your own desire. It's perfectly natural."

His control was back now, his calm pride restored with what he thought of as his knowledge.

"That's not why I held the sign up," I said, weakly. I knew that wasn't why I held the sign up, and I knew he'd never really believe a word I said, even if I could find the words, which I could not. So I rode along, letting him think what he wanted. I felt sorry for him now, having seen who he was without the cloak of his composure.

I didn't go back to the darkroom anymore, or even to violin lessons. I gave the excuse that I had to do a lot of work for my mother. But maybe Horace had some kind of clue as to why I quit. I saw him four months later downtown, on a stark autumn afternoon. I was walking a rich man's dog for two dollars. I wore an old T-shirt and jeans and a sweatshirt tied around my waist.

"How are you?" he said. His eyes seemed less forceful, less knowing as he looked at me. I was glad to see him.

"I'm fine. How's Rosa?"

"Fine. Everything's fine. So is that your dog?"

"No. I got a temporary job as a dog walker," I said.

"Not a bad job," he said.

"No, and the dog's nice."

An awkward silence fell.

"I might not ever see you again. Would you mind if I took your picture?" he said.

"Sure."

I leaned back against the red side wall of Woolworth's, sad, somehow, but comfortable, as I heard the shutter close.

Eyes of Others

....

> Frank said, glancing at the children in the rearview, "I don't need no backseat drivers." Corrine, Frank's wife, said, "Maybe you need another frontseat driver?" She'd tried to say this warmly, then smiled over at him, her face already lined, worn looking, though she was a mere thirty-nine. Her hair, newly dyed red, was cut in a bowl shape, and she'd tried to curl it back to make a frame for her face like the rolled-back brim on the sort of hats that looked good on her. Now the curls were loosening, falling forward into her eyes. She fought off the urge to take this as an omen.

Frank peered ahead at the road in a sort of concentrated boredom, as if there would be no surprises, no turns or swerves—and yet the road itself was one long, swerving turn, one snakelike, curving, narrow surprise of a mountain road, and Corrine thought, Should I be scared? Should I feel my heart leap when the car gets too close to the cliff and Frank doesn't seem to notice? She was aware of something inside of her trusting Frank, trusting wholly and heavily, and also aware lately that this trust sprung from a deep passivity, a resignation she'd made—when? She didn't know.

Now she watched bare, black trees clawing the red skyline and for a moment felt scared of the sky's beauty. "Look at this sunset," she said. Frank didn't look. Motion. Moving. Keep this car going. Sometimes she felt that being a passenger was the most interesting privilege the world afforded. It was in a car that she felt most at home.

"Things look better when you're passing them by," she said, then laughed. Frank looked over at her, then back at the road.

The children whom Frank had warned not to backseat drive were both nine years old. The boy was Corrine's and the girl was Frank's, yet they looked strangely related, both of them wiry, dark-eyed, and pale. And the expressions that passed heavily over their faces—now astonishment, now sadness, now that raw look of accusation, sometimes seemed like expressions they planned together, a conspiratorial symmetry. In the beginning, that symmetry had seemed to Corrine a fact to add to her list of why she and Frank should be together.

"I'm hungry," Frank said. They were heading for a tunnel.

"I am too," Corrine said. "Kids?"

She looked back and watched them shake their heads sleepily. As they entered the tunnel the car filled up with light, and the children looked like they'd been plugged in.

"Are we honestly under a mountain right now?" said the girl, Helen. Corrine had noticed that "honestly" was Helen's favorite word.

"Hell yes," Frank said. "Can't you feel it?"

The boy, Kyle John, tried to whistle in appreciation. "If the tunnel caved in on us, we'd all be crushed dead, you know. We'd go up to heaven and Michael Archangel will look at us and say, "Were you kind?"

"Honey," Corrine said. "Michael knows. He won't have to ask you a thing. He's an archangel."

"What a load of bullshit that is," Frank said.

"Frank, you—"

"Scaring that boy to death as if he don't have enough to fear right here on planet earth."

Frank was always calling it "planet earth." It made him sound like a man well-traveled, a man who compared this world to the last one he'd seen.

Suddenly Corrine wanted to please him. Moments like this would grip her, and she'd believe that if she didn't please Frank somehow, everything would begin to slowly collapse.

"Kyle John, you know Michael Archangel's maybe not a real angel, don't you?"

"No."

"And heaven, heaven's just a state of mind." She turned around to the backseat; the children stared at her. She turned back around.

The tunnel ended abruptly, purple dusk light instantly flooding the car. It was a new and deeper silence Frank spoke into. "We'll get off this road and hit the pike," he said.

Then Helen started singing. She had a high, clear voice and knew the words to hundreds of songs, pop songs she found on the radio or on Frank's scratchy records. Corrine turned to watch her sing.

"I bless the day I found you. / I'm gonna build my whole world around you. . . ."

She was so unlike Frank, Corrine thought, seeing the girl washed by headlights of a passing car. She must get those shining eyes from her mother. Corrine had never seen the woman, save for in a photograph she found in the glove compartment, and in that black-and-white snapshot the woman stood on an empty beach in a black one-piece bathing suit and a silver ankle bracelet. She made the beach look cold somehow, as if it were late autumn. The picture had been enough to set Corrine's reluctant imagination reeling. On the back of it she'd written, "Remember this day, Frankie." Once Corrine dreamed the woman was twirling in circles in a barren room with Frank outside peering in through a blue window.

....

"I'm gonna do everything for you / A man could want a girl to do. . . ."

Corrine tried to conjure up an image of her ex-husband, a memory of her own to hold against Frank's past, which rose in her chest like a dark wave that wouldn't break. But whenever she thought of him, he was wearing that purple shirt with the pineapples, the ugly one he'd made uglier by wearing it on the back porch the night he'd looked into her eyes, all his patience and pity gone, and said, "Can't you understand I just don't feel it anymore?"

"She can really sing," Corrine told Frank. He looked over at her and smiled—or rather his mouth smiled. The rest of his face seemed lost in some private dark that Corrine sometimes felt like she was traveling toward.

Now, in Howard Johnson's, they sat in a booth—Frank and Helen on one side, Corrine and Kyle John on the other. Kyle John was reading aloud from the dessert menu, stumbling over words Corrine felt he should know. He said "Chocolate sigh-rup," and Corrine said, "The word's *syrup*, Kyle. What grade are you in?"

The waitress appeared at the table's edge, a serious woman ready to write on her pad.

"These two want the spaghetti special," Frank told her, "and the lady here will have the fish and green beans. And I'll have your Salisbury steak and whatever comes with it."

"Fried or mashed?"

"Mashed," Frank said. "No, make it fried."

Corrine felt a rush of warmth pass through her. Frank's moments of indecision were so rare that when they came about he looked vulnerable.

Before the food came, Frank said, "The closer we get, the more sure I am that I won't go knocking on the door and ask to see inside."

"Oh really? But I wanted to see your boyhood bedroom."

Frank waved his hand through the air. "It ain't my boyhood bedroom anyhow. Not anymore."

"So we came four hours just for the outside view?" Corrine said.

"You're getting a change of scenery out of the deal, right?"

"Sure. But you know me, I was just looking forward to seeing the rooms you walked around in when you were small. I'm just that way."

Corrine didn't know much about how Frank grew up; either he wasn't inclined to remember, or he withheld his past for reasons of his own. But one night he'd said, when they were eating salad, "My mother loved radishes. I can still see her washing them off in the sink. She grew them every damn year. Big old radish garden."

Corrine had held her breath, hoping that he would go on and say something else. But that was it. An entire kitchen—square with white curtains and work boots on a mat by the door—had formed itself in Corrine's mind as he spoke, and the woman washing radishes had looked over her shoulder with surprised green eyes.

Their dinners were served now, and everyone ate in silence for a while. Then Helen began laughing.

"What?"

"What is it, Helen?"

"Tell us what's funny."

She couldn't stop laughing to speak. Her face was bright red, and tears began to stream from her eyes. And when she tried to speak she nearly choked on her food so that Frank had to pat her on the back, his hand enormous looking because she was so small. He gave her a drink of water and they all watched her drink and begin to calm down, her eyes wide and wet.

"Tell us what you were laughing about," Corrine said, smiling.

Helen began twirling her spaghetti. She took a deep breath.

....

"Come on, what was so funny?" Corrine said. She wanted to laugh herself, she wanted everyone to laugh together.

"One time at Acme Mom pretended she was a big duck," the girl said, then bit her lip and hid her eyes behind her hands.

The car was an old '67 Malibu in excellent shape. The inside of it was spacious, the seats blue-and-white plaid, untorn, the outside a sleek shade of navy that looked black in the night. It was Corrine's car, the one her first husband had bought for six hundred dollars and fixed up. Frank called it "the Bomb," and yet it ran better than his Impala, which was only two years old. They were back on the mountain road now, and Corrine pointed the stars out to the children.

"I bet you didn't know there were so many," she said. "It looks like there's more stars than sky."

Even Frank looked up every other minute or so in a sort of awe. Some of the stars were so low it looked like they would have to drive through them.

"When I was a boy, I slept outside and stared up at skies like this for hours," Frank said.

"You honestly used to sleep outside?" Helen said, sitting up, one of her hands patting the hair that fell shaggily onto her father's neck.

"Sure I did. We all slept out. There weren't so many maniacs back then."

Corrine reached over and put her hand on his knee.

"Can me and Kyle John sleep out sometime?" Helen said.

Frank laughed. "Sure, right there on that nice concrete slab we call the backyard. Hogan's killer dog would have you kids for a midnight snack to save you from getting kidnapped."

Helen sat back. The stars kept getting brighter, closer, more plentiful as they rose. Corrine said, "Who can see all this and not believe in God?"

Frank said, "Me."

They were on a small dirt road now. Pebbles shot up under the car and clinked. Trees on either side of the road twisted into the bright night air.

"This is my road, by the way," Frank said. "And we're coming up on my house." He cleared his throat.

The house was at the dead end of the road, and now they were stopped before it. It was dark brick with two chimneys and a front porch. Frank turned on the high beams. There was a single light on in an upstairs window, and a dark human shape passed before it, then appeared again, stopped, and stared down at them.

"This is it?" Helen said.

It was an old man up there, and he pressed his forehead to the window now.

"This is it?" Helen repeated.

"Of course this is it. Why else would I sit here like an idiot with my high beams on?"

The old man pulled open the window and leaned out. Frank got out of the car, and Corrine rolled her window down. The man called out, "Is there car trouble?"

"No sir," Frank said.

"You need a telephone?" the man called down.

"No, I don't. I don't need—I used to live here in this house. Just came back to show the wife and kids, you know."

"You lived here? When was that?"

"A million years ago," Frank said, and laughed. "Thanks a lot now, I have to be going."

"Wait!" the man cried.

Frank turned around and looked up at him. The old man waved him in. "Come on in and see if it's changed. Bring everyone on in."

"No, no, that's fine," Frank said, and walked back and got into the car. He started up the engine and looked once more at the house. The man was gone from the window. But as Frank backed the car up, the man appeared on the steps of the porch, waving them in with all his might. "Hey Frank," Corrine said. "He really wants us to come in." Frank looked in the rearview. Now they could hear the old man shouting, "I'll give you a warm drink! Whatever you like! Please!"

Frank turned the car away from the house now, dirt clouds rising in the air behind him, both children kneeling to look out the back window. The man was chasing after them. ·

"Stop, Frank! He's chasing us, he's running after us."

Frank would not slow down.

Helen began to cry. "We should stop!" she kept saying, long after the old man was out of sight.

Trust, that had been so thorough on the way up, crumbled on the way down, though the actual driving had improved, and Frank seemed to anxiously take note each time the road got smaller or curved.

Every family outing seemed to fail somehow. They'd gone to Great Adventure last spring and baboons had jumped all over Frank's car. They'd gone to Manuel's, a famous Mexican restaurant, and Kyle had tripped and cracked his head open on the edge of a table. At the Jersey shore last year, where they'd rented a house for a whole week, dolphins were washing up on the beach amid hospital waste—bags of blood, syringes, old rubber gloves, rusty scalpels and a lot of things they couldn't name. They'd tried to sit on the beach, ignoring it all. The next trip to the beach was in early October, when they'd nearly had the place to themselves. Corrine had imagined she and Frank would sit in chairs, soaking up the year's last real sun, their feet burrowing into the sand, watching the children swim, chatting or flipping through magazines, then eating the lunch she packed.

Corrine stared at the brilliant stars and remembered that lunch—the fried chicken, celery stalks with cream cheese and paprika, grape juice, banana cake, the six of beer. She closed her eyes now and saw it all wrapped, the perfect way she had fit everything snugly into the cooler.

But Frank that day, after drinking half the beer before noon, had told her, "Think I'll go for a little stroll," and kissed the part in her hair before walking off. She could remember smiling up at him, him smiling down at her, the memory of desire still in their eyes, her stomach twisting into a knot.

"I'll stay here and watch the kids," she told him, as if there'd been a choice. She'd turned and watched him walk down the boardwalk, most of the shops closed up, hardly any people around. She had feared that he would keep on walking until he found himself another life. How easy that would be for him! Even in the distance he looked big to her—tall, strong, a solitary man nobody would diminish.

They'd searched all day before they found him in a bar, watching a ball game on TV, flocked by other men. She could still see his face when she walked up behind him and tapped his back. She remembered how tight her skin felt, how her hair was sandy and tangled, her lips chapped, her nose greased with sunscreen, and how he'd looked at her as if she were a stranger. That very look seemed to have the power to turn her into one.

"I think from now on I want to stay home," Corrine said now. Frank sighed. She looked into the backseat where the children had fallen asleep, each one of their heads against a door.

"It was awful, driving away from that old man," Corrine said.

"Oh come on, he could've been crazy for all we know."

Corrine closed her eyes, and images of her first husband swirled through her mind. He would have stopped for that old man; they would have gone in and stayed for a long time. She saw her husband standing on the beach with Kyle asleep on a blanket in the shade of his leg. When the image collapsed in on itself and left a cold hole behind her breastbone, she opened her eyes to the dark.

"Frank?"

"Mmmm?"

"I'm hungry. Could we get dessert? The dessert we didn't have after dinner?"

He looked at his watch. "Sure," he said. "What the hell."

He reached over and patted her leg. She took both of her hands and grabbed his and held it there, tears in her eyes like thick shields blurring the lights of the car in front of them.

"Wake up, Kyle, Helen. Time to wake up and eat some dessert," she told them. Frank was out in the parking lot stretching under the harsh lights that gave the air a metallic, greenish tint.

"I'm not hungry," Helen said, her eyes still closed. Kyle John pouted and blinked, staring up at Corrine. "Where am I?" he said.

"Come on now, kids," Corrine coaxed softly. She was beginning to regret this dessert idea; it seemed cruel to wake these children like this. She looked over at Frank again, who stood with his arms crossed, watching a man step down out of an eighteen-wheeler.

"We'll have chocolate sundaes," Corrine said. But when Kyle closed his eyes again she lost patience. "Come on," she snapped, "Both of you wake up. You can sleep when you're dead." She nudged their shoulders.

The children each opened their door and nearly fell out of the car. In the lot they stood and groaned about the cold and Frank called over that he didn't want to hear it.

"Don't complain, don't explain," he hollered. It was one of his favorite sayings.

Now he held the glass door open and they all filed into the restaurant. This Howard Johnson's was spanking new, everything brown and rust colored instead of the classic orange and turquoise. It was a disappointment.

The children looked startlingly awake now, but that was the way it was with children; they looked both more asleep and more awake, as if the border between these two states shrunk with age.

Both children ordered clown sundaes. Frank got a banana split. Corrine, suddenly weight-conscious, ordered split-pea soup.

"Excuse me, I have to go to the ladies," she said before the food arrived. In the blue-tiled bathroom another woman was at the sink washing her hands. Corrine went into a stall and waited for the woman to leave. She wanted to reapply her make-up, but needed privacy; how some people could stand in public encountering their own eyes in the mirror while others watched Corrine would never know.

When the woman was gone, Corrine slipped out of the stall. She stood next to the mirror and dug up foundation, lipstick, and mascara from her purse. She applied only the foundation; she didn't want this to be too obvious. Then she practiced smiling at the mirror, as if the mirror were Frank.

When the food arrived, Corrine looked out the window that lined the booth, past her own reflection to the parking lot. A few stranded-looking trees tossed in the wind as if a storm might be coming. A small child in a white coat was standing under one of the lights, her arms folded, her foot in a western boot, tapping.

"Corrine, this was a great idea," Frank said. "Really."

A part of her that had sunk inside now fought its way up to the surface like a small animal. She smiled what she knew to be her prettiest smile, and Frank winked, but it left her cold.

Helen and Kyle were engrossed in their clown sundaes which had arrived on long metal plates. Corrine began to eat her soup and became aware of a woman across the aisle. She was alone, eating pancakes and drinking a glass of burgundy. She wore a very outdated paisley dress—the colors were harsh greens and blues. She was hunched over her food so that her thin black hair fell toward it. Corrine got a glance at her legs under the table—dark nylons leading to old-fashioned red shoes. For some reason, Corrine's heart lurched forward at the sight of the shoes.

"Did I ever see a real clown, Mom?" Kyle John said.

"You did," she said. "You went to the circus. Don't you remember?"

"Nope."

"You had a great time."

"Did I ever see a real clown, Dad?"

Corrine watched the woman's sharp, snow white elbow jutting out as the woman cut into her pancakes. The woman paused suddenly, put down her fork, and pushed her hair behind her ear—a curtain pulled back for Corrine. Corrine stared at the profile, the skin white as sheets, the unblinking eyes staring ahead as if transfixed by something she suddenly recalled. Then the woman sucked in her cheeks and arched her neck up and stared at the ceiling as if in a daze. She stayed that way for a few seconds, Corrine holding her in her peripheral vision. Frank was in the middle of a story about what happened to Helen the day she'd been to the circus—she'd gotten lost and ended up in the wrong section with an old lady and her grown-up son. "I went crazy looking for you, and when I found you you smiled and said, "Hi, Daddy!" You didn't even know you were lost."

"No!" Helen said, and began to laugh her side-splitting laugh.

A man stood in front of the woman across the aisle now. The back of him was tall and broad-shouldered in a black windbreaker. He was blocking Corrine's view of the woman's face.

Then the man bent down and kissed the woman on the cheek, then on the lips, and slid into the seat across from her. Corrine heard him say, "Pancakes and burgundy?"

"I got lost once, but really I ran away," Kyle John was saying. "Remember, Mom?"

"Yes," she said. She didn't turn and stare directly at the couple, but she could see them from the corner of her eye. They didn't speak. They simply looked at each other.

"Tell that story, Kyle John," Corrine said, and as she spoke she found a way to look over at them without it seeming rude. She pretended to be looking just over their heads.

Their eyes were locked together, their smiles restrained and intensely private. Kyle John must have said something funny, for even Frank had exploded into laughter. The couple would not look away from each other. "What else?" Frank was saying.

"It's true, right Mom?" Kyle John said.

"Every word," Corrine answered, to what she didn't know. How did they meet? she was thinking now. How long ago? What did they talk about before they slept? She thought she could see their bed by a window. She thought they had been through hell together.

The woman finished her meal, still looking at the man as she ate. At one point they laughed, and the man said something Corrine couldn't hear, and then they resumed looking at each other.

They rose to go. The woman's coat was as strange as her dress—a flowered coat like someone might wear at Eastertime in 1950. As she slipped into it, her eyes did not leave his.

They walked up to the register and stood side by side, waiting to pay. Corrine was not ready to lose them.

"I need some gum," she announced, and got out of the booth and headed toward the couple. She stood in back of them as they paid, breathing in their smell, a mysterious and all-encompassing smell like that of another season. Corrine

....

looked into her purse, pretending to search for coins, then looked up, just a few inches from the billowing flowers on the narrow back of the Easter coat. And then the sound of the register slamming, the cashier saying "Good-night now," the couple turning and walking out the door, and Corrine following behind them, distant enough to be inconspicuous, close enough to hear what they might say to each other. But they didn't speak, or even hold hands, just kept walking inside of their incredible sheltering silence, heading to their gray car.

"Excuse me!" Corrine yelled. She had shocked herself. The couple turned and faced her. They stared at her, waiting, puzzled. Corrine stood a few yards away now, and could not think of what to ask them.

"You dropped this," she finally said, and dug frantically into her purse for some money. She brought out a limp five-dollar bill, one corner of it streaked with lipstick.

The man stepped up and took it from her, nodding, and then his voice, deep and straightforward, thanked her.

"It was real nice of you to follow us out here in this cold," the woman called, her strange white face breaking into a smile before she slipped into the car and shut the door.

"Mom!" came the voice of Kyle John, ringing in the air behind her. "Frank wants to know what you're doing outside!"

While Mother Was Gone with 571

....

➤ Last night my mother had her first date with 571. She has a big case on him, so she wore the beige dress with the ivy vines slinking all over it. And orange fishnet stockings on her legs. You could look at her face and know she knew what a knock-out she was.

My sister and I call him 571 because that's what his license plate says. He's a doctor and very short. About as big as the floor fan that's always spinning in the corner of our upstairs hall. Mother's had a huge case on him for months, or maybe longer, you never know. She used to come into our room in the morning and say to my sister, "Katherine, you look so pale and wan. Maybe you best stay home from school today if you're not up to par." And Katherine knew as well as I did that Mother wanted to cart her off to see 571. But unlike me Katherine hates school worse than doctors. She's in ninth at Our Lady of the Seven Sorrows, and I'm in sixth at Immaculate Heart. Our Lady of the Seven is twice as hard, strict, and boring as Immaculate Heart. So Katherine would look at my mother and say, "Yes, I do feel sick." Then she'd hold her stomach and groan to make it seem less of a lie to us all. I'd say, "OK, you two, have fun visiting 571." Then I'd slip on my uniform and storm outside as soon as possible and head down to school for boredom.

....

My mother would sure enough get spruced up and take Katherine to his little brick doctor office on Tenth and Broom. I can see Katherine trying to look ill and my mother in one of the flower dresses and her long lips painted red, sitting ladylike on the stool in the corner of the examining room by the window while 571 holds a stethoscope on the bare chest of Katherine, saying, "Breathe deep." I can picture 571 saying, "Why Katherine here is just as healthy as the days are long," and my mother saying that it's probably just a case of tiredness and growing pains, then giving him one of her smiles. She's a tall redhead with movie star teeth and all curves. She smokes menthols all day long and people like to watch her. On the inhale her eyebrows come together like she's working on a problem, on the exhale they relax like the problem's been solved. People always tell her, "You look good when you smoke." And it's a good thing she does since she'd smoke in her sleep if she could. It's really something to drive with her, since she's got one hand on the wheel while the other holds the Benson & Hedges, not to mention the habit of her mind to wander so far she doesn't see she's about to smash into the green sidewall of J. Kustler Bakery, which we came close to doing last Tuesday.

After my father left, my mother took to tooling around in the Ford. We'd go with her because she always wants people to go with her. I soon figured out that we were following 571 around town. It was a little like a spy movie. 571 drives a light blue brand-new '65 Corvair, and we'd all be craning our necks to spot it. You could look down an alley sometimes and see it sliding by. The one time we managed to get beside him at a red light, my mother froze up and wouldn't even look over at him until the light changed and he pulled away, then she almost fell out of the car waving at him. He saw her in the rearview and stuck his arm out of his window and waved back. My mother threw her head back and laughed like this was very clever of him. I could go on and on about all the accidents we had just trying to catch up with the man. That's why I'm glad he and my mother had a date. Now she won't have to risk our lives. Though I might be going away for a while anyhow with Arlene Thompkins, a friend of mine who knows Atlantic City and whose brother Louis lives there in a room with the ocean for a front yard.

Anyhow, not only did my mother have a date last night, Katherine had one. My mother said she couldn't have one until she was fifteen, then backed down and said all right. Katherine teased up her yellow hair, using six tons of Adorn hair spray, and wore my mother's white sandals with the heels. She put on a red skirt with a jacket to match. On the jacket is somebody else's monogram; she didn't care, she looked about seventeen.

Arlene Thompkins and I just sat there on the couch in the living room while Mother and Katherine waited for their dates. The windows were open, and the late sunlight streamed in, lighting up my mother, who sat facing the front door in the blue chair like a queen. There was a breeze in the curtains which only made the rest of the room too still. Even my mother got very quiet. Then Arlene started laughing for no reason. The harder she tried not to laugh the more she laughed, and then I was laughing, too, since it was contagious. My mother and Katherine were just looking at us. "Did somebody tell a joke?" my mother said to Katherine with a raised eyebrow. When I elbowed Arlene, she jumped, and her blue glasses flew off her face onto the floor. She gave me a disgusted look, then all of a sudden a knock came at the door; a soft little knock which made me know it was old 571, and my mother must've known too. She leaped out of the chair, grabbed her shawl from the banister, told us to be good and she wouldn't be late and not to go into her room or eat all the marble cake. Then she swung the storm door open, and I watched at the window as 571 stepped back. He was casually dressed in a windbreaker. My mother said, "Well, Johnny, hello!" Then she linked his arm and practically dragged him down the walkway to his Corvair, parked on the curb crookedly. They got in the car, and he drove her away politely.

Soon after, Edwin Sculley came for Katherine. Arlene's eyes came out of their sockets when he walked in. He's a basketball player, very handsome in some people's opinion. Katherine was nervous and smiling, and you could tell she was dying to get away from the house. Edwin told her she looked nice and stared at her stacked top while Arlene and I stared at him from the couch, not missing anything. He looked at us and said, "You two look awful happy. Got something up your sleeve?" I shook my head "no," thinking, Don't I wish, and Katherine winked and said, "Good-night, girls." Edwin Sculley said not to do anything he wouldn't do, and then they were gone out the door, and it was just me and Arlene on the couch like two old ladies at a bus stop. We sat and listened to Edwin Sculley's car move down West Twenty-seventh. Then it was quiet.

I stood up. "Now what?" I said.

Arlene shrugged. "Beats me," she said.

One thing I was not in the mood for was laughing about Edwin Sculley and Katherine, so when Arlene started up, I said, "Lets act our age and not our shoe size." Then I started walking up to my room, Arlene clumping behind. I sat down on my bed, and she sat down on Katherine's bed, facing me. We looked at each other. Then we got up and both of us were walking downstairs, not saying anything. We walked right outside and the McCabe boys were fooling around on their porch and Francine Yarmey was doing the Hula Hoop and a lot of other kids were on the curb sucking freeze pops. I pulled my blue Super Ball out of my pocket, and we walked out to the middle of the street. I like being in the middle of the street. It's long and all the houses on both sides are connected like walls, so you can feel like you're in a decent hallway with the sky for a ceiling. I bounced the ball to Arlene and we had ourselves a catch, ignoring their comments about Lard (Arlene) and the pencil-necked geek (me).

Two doors down on the opposite side of the street from our house, I could see Rose Pellerzy with her old watering can sprinkling the spider mums in her front yard. Kids hate her because she tells you to get off her lawn even if you have to fetch something you've lost, like your shoe or a ball. She has a mean, shaking kind of voice. Michael Fiorelli says she's a witch. He even saw her through her window one night all dressed in black and pacing back and forth in her kitchen. She's not even too old. About thirty-seven going on thirty-eight. But she's skinny as an old lady, with hunched shoulders and no husband or even boyfriend. Probably as skinny as me. And her hair is another story, just hanging there.

So we had ourselves a catch, and I watched Rose Pellerzy and thought of this idea. I turned it around in my head, and the more I thought about it, the funnier I thought it was. I stopped the catch and told Arlene to come sit on the curb so I could tell her the idea. I said wouldn't it be great to call a cab and say we were Rose Pellerzy and that we needed to go somewhere right away. Arlene said she thought that was a great idea. So we got into my house and got the telephone book out. I looked up "Taxi," and there were about seven or eight companies in the city. Then I got the idea that we wouldn't only call *one* company. We'd call a whole *bunch*. I figured we could time it so that a cab showed up at her house every ten minutes for an hour or something. I figured we could go right up on our roof and watch the whole thing. I told the plan to Arlene.

We called four cab companies. Lincoln, City Cab, Otto's, and Hillman Brothers. To each man that we talked to, I said, "Hello, my name is Rose Pellerzy. I live at 16 West Twenty-

....

seventh, and I need a cab because I'm going on an outing to Philadelphia for some dancing and dining." Then I'd tell him a time. At first, Arlene was cracking up and had to leave the room and fall on the floor in the hallway. I started laughing, too, at one point and had to hang up on Hillman Brothers and call back a few minutes later in a lower voice.

After we made our phone calls, we went up on the roof. There were a lot of stars out and an orange moon. Down on the corner kids were playing freeze tag, and we could hear Jimmy McCabe trying to boss the world around as usual. Arlene and I just sat there and waited until finally the first cab came. It sat and beeped smack in front of Rose Pellerzy's. She came out on her porch wearing what looked like a man's raincoat, but I thought maybe it was a bathrobe. She stood on her porch with her hand above her eyes the way captains do on boats. The driver got out of the car and said, "What's the holdup?" He was fat, with his hands on his hips. Rose Pellerzy said, "I think you must have the wrong house number. Perhaps you wanted the McCabes, next door?" The driver asked her if the number on her house was sixteen, and she said, "Yes, it is." He stood there staring at her for a minute, shrugged, then got in his cab and drove away with his arm hanging out the window and tapping the door. We were up there laughing. It was like watching a movie where you know what's going to happen but not exactly.

When the next cab came, the horn was very loud. Louder than the first. Rose Pellerzy came out on her porch again and made a go away sign with her arm. The driver just kept beeping. And she just kept waving him away, but it was like he wouldn't take no for an answer. So Rose Pellerzy walked off her porch and out to the curb and said, "I didn't ask for you. I'm not going anywhere." The driver rolled down his window and said, "Watzat you say there, lady?" We could hear the song "Moon River" coming out of the cab. Rose Pellerzy said again, "I didn't ask for you. I'm not going anywhere. Go away now, go on." So he said, "Whadda ya mean, ya change your mind?" and she said, "I don't know what the mix-up is, but, really, I haven't any need for your services." Her voice was even shakier than usual. "Well," the cab driver said, "Anything you say, lady." Then he pulled away, making a loud screech. He practically turned the corner on two wheels up where they were now playing relievio and somebody yelled after him, "Slow down, you ignorant pig!" while other kids shouted some worse things that you can imagine.

It seemed like a long time before the third cab came. It was getting a little chilly, so I climbed through the window and got two of Katherine's sweaters out of the cedar chest. I brought them back to the roof and we put them on. They smelled like the cedar chest and Katherine's perfume.

Arlene and I talked about stars, light-years, galaxies, outer space, how all the stars were basically just rushing away from us at four million miles an hour. Once when I told my mother this fact, she said, "Can you blame them?"

We put our heads back on the roof and enjoyed the view. When we looked back down at the houses on the street, they looked for a second like toys.

When the third cab came, the driver beeped as usual. After the third beep, Rose Pellerzy ran out of her house like a woman gone out of control. She flapped her arms and screamed, *"I did not call for you! I do not need you! Go! Go!"* Arlene and I just stared. We saw Mrs. McCabe and Mr. Smentkowski on their porches, looking at Rose Pellerzy and probably wondering if they should go over and see what was happening. But they didn't. The driver shouted from the window, "OK, lady, for cryin' out loud, I hear ya!" But Rose Pellerzy didn't seem to hear him, and she shouted back, *"I do not need you! Get out of here now!"* It sounded like she was starting to cry. *"Now!"* she kept saying. I was getting scared now and thinking what would happen when another cab showed up. I couldn't remember which company showed up yet, so I couldn't even call and tell them please not to come.

The driver got out of the cab. "Pull yourself together, ma'am, it's just a mistake," he said, and Rose Pellerzy looked at him, then looked up and down the street. It was a raincoat she was wearing. She walked inside and flicked off her porch light. The driver got into his car and left. Mr. Smentkowski walked over and started talking to Mrs. McCabe on her porch.

We watched as all the lights went out in Rose Pellerzy's house. Then we climbed through the window and walked through the bedroom and downstairs.

Arlene said, "What about the next cab?" and I didn't say anything. I cut giant slices of cake and poured us each a glass of cold milk. We took them into the other room and ate them on the couch.

When the fourth cab showed up and beeped, I walked to the storm door and stared out through the screen into the dark. There was no sign of Rose Pellerzy, not even a light flicking on. The cab waited a minute or so, then drove off.

I walked back to the couch and finished my milk and asked Arlene to take off my sister's sweater. Then I said I was tired and asked her if she could go home. "Sure," she said. "Whatever." She took her plate and glass out to the kitchen and left by the back door. I stood at the window and watched her cut through the alley in her scooter skirt and felt bad I'd asked her to leave.

I went up to my room and didn't turn any lights on. I took off my clothes and put on my nightgown. Then I knelt by the window and looked across the street at Rose Pellerzy's house for a long time. I closed my eyes and thought about my father and how I didn't know where he was. I couldn't even picture where he might be, which was the worst part. A person needs to picture where other people are. I listened to parents ringing bells because it was time for everyone to come in. I listened to kids asking if they could stay outside for five more minutes. Then I stood up and got into my bed. I lay there perfectly still under the cold sheet, with a view of all those stars.

Thirst

....

➤ It was the time of the fish.

It was the time of the fish and the pale blue house and the field of yellow reeds. Wind from the river rose up the hill like steep, translucent waves, then crashed through the field, sending reeds earthward, all of them rooted dancers flying together, never wholly aligned with earth but leaning, leaning, then suddenly standing up straight in the absence of wind. At night the moon poured into the reeds, giving them protection made of clear, white light, the bending and swaying inside of that light as if inside a room one sees in a dream.

Inside the house Doris's head rested on top of her unusually long neck, and she carried it like a crystal on a stand that might roll off if tilted. She would sigh, a tall woman encircled in a secrecy that swirled around her like a current, provoking desire. William was the one who'd gotten through.

Heat from the black Franklin stove rippled over her thighs during this time of the fish and the pale blue house, the reeds and now the new child, a three-year-old girl they had picked up one day like groceries, William driving white-faced in the maroon interior, his hands strong on the jagged wheel, while Doris held the package on her wide woolen lap with a fixed smile on her face. The child, not yet named, cried quietly and looked out the window toward strangers in other cars.

But soon after they were home, Doris thought of the child falling and cutting her head on the corner of the black slate slab upon which the stove stood, blood gushing on the blonde head, small bruises spreading over the stunned face like insects. And she would dream the child was only a dream, that in the morning she might wake to walk into what they'd converted into a child's bedroom and find it William's study again, a serious place, Kokoschka prints, voluminous books, a giant cactus, his collection of bone-colored antlers on the wide sills, and all the blue bears tumbling down the walls, gone forever.

But nothing was ever a dream, not even a dream, and William named the child Sasha. And Sasha turned four, the tap-dancing age, her dimpled knees ready, winking. Doris drove her to the lessons, picturing herself stopping the car suddenly by the river and throwing the child in, an image untended, unrecognized even, gone for good to the land where such thoughts gather to wait for the time of return.

Were a stranger to confess imagining something similar, Doris would have felt a dim sense of recall, wondered if she'd seen a movie about such a thing. And then she'd walk away from the stranger, horrified, though in those years she would never have met the stranger to begin with. Doris preferred remaining at home in the blue house, painting and cleaning, arranging things, looking out the window. She called the fish inside of her a cramp, and felt it rarely.

Doris, whose arms were strong, found the child nearly impossible to lift, never suspecting in these years the weight of darkness she herself had poured into that essence, fears hardening in the heat of the child so that when she could not lift Sasha, it was herself that had become too heavy to hold. The tail of the fish would rise, an internal tickle, nearly noticed. Sometimes Doris would bend down and hold her mouth an inch away from the child's temple and say her name, *Sasha,* imagining the warm circle of breath that settled under the word as if to catch it, protect the child, the naming itself a weapon.

Meanwhile, William played the white piano in the red room behind the kitchen, music weak and futile to the ears of Doris, though he kept saying he was improving, exploring new territory. The sound searched in lame meander, never a crescendo. Get to the point, she'd think, and the tinkling of the high notes would answer her like mockery, music proclaiming there is no destination, but look at the pathways for fingers—how infinite can you get?

Sometimes the child would sleep with her head on Doris's lap, and Doris would sit watching the river wind snap down the reeds, her arms crossed, one foot tapping on the thick blue carpet, a soft thud marking time. The reeds framed in the window rose up and stood still, a line of starved soldiers standing at attention, and Doris would try to smile for William, sensing him suddenly in the doorway, a man with a dark beard and horn-rimmed glasses, tall in the loose clothes that disguised him—the firmest skin over sculpted muscle and bone. There were times in the morning when he would be dressing, and she would glance up to find the back of him suddenly facing her with a male beauty so pure it was always an affront; it was almost a face, as if between the shoulder blades were sudden black eyes. And the desire that flared inside of her came hot and spliced with a paralyzing violence she refused to acknowledge even as her teeth clenched against it. She would not move; she would not even breathe. Her mind clung like a bat to a high corner of itself where a voice said she was nice, a gentle woman with some talent, a husband, a child—while under her skin she continued to burn, waiting for the clothes to cover him, the dangerous element of desire vanishing with that covering. Then she would move out of the room away from all that, calling back over her shoulder through the crooked blue hall, "Care for some tomato juice?" But the hard, tapered beauty, the bone and ease of it that would never be completely hers, though she desired it more than life itself, would leave a hole in her each time she walked away from it, and often, though she never felt this, the fish would leap through the hole, testing its size.

And so in the doorways William continued to lean, his face the face of a man watching his wife and child, never wondering why the wife's arms were crossed. Or why she spoke to Sasha as if she were an adult and should understand everything. Doris would remember the first day the three of them had lived together, how she had voiced a shrill excitement to cover up regret, while he had quietly studied the child, amazed at the tiny hands that tried to clap and missed themselves. And in the child's eyes there was fright and beauty and a critical blue distance, a certain severity that made William laugh right from the beginning. "She's a reincarnation of someone. Maybe not Kafka, but that original," he said, and then, as if the three year old had grasped perfectly the meaning of his words, she laughed, a sound like a hiccup, the lips curling up and settling back into their reserve. She clapped again, didn't miss this time, the fingers splaying childishly in every direction, the sound of the clap like a kiss.

William had lifted her into the air above him, staring up through raining sun into her face while Doris had watched his soul in these moments adopt the child with a love she never dreamed possible. So easily won. Sasha laughed again—brook water—her large eyes on the eyes of her father, the air between their gazing as wavy as heat. Then he twirled her, laughing with so much pleasure that Doris had to say, "Here, let me hold her, you'll hurt her." But opening her trembling arms to receive the reluctant child, something in her chest clanged shut like the door of a cell. She felt the reverberations of that closing throughout her body as the child spoke her first words that the house had to hold, an insistent *Down,* and then, *I want down,* and the room itself seemed to sink.

"Sometimes this feels like a houseboat," William said one afternoon, smiling by the window, noticing nothing, no longer caring that what he once thought of as his indestructible passion—the study of primitive societies—was being squelched by department politics, no longer caring that he was growing bored and unimportant in the field where he'd so hoped to make a mark.

He and Sasha named every blue bear on the wall beside her bed in the moonlight and then made up stories about a few of them. The stories continued from one night to the next, through the years. And Doris would lie reading hardbacks down the hall, window across from the high bed opened on the cool nights in spring, the curtains rounding as a pregnant stomach with dark wind, then flattening suddenly, sucked hungrily against the screen.

William, later, would pull her toward his body on the bed, smelling of trees or chopped lumber and fire, his hands discovering the layers of her hair that she felt then as extensions of her mind, chestnut thoughts, smooth and stretching out, limited and unknowable. Falling into the hole in that double bed's center, falling and wanting him to pull her hair harder, she knew the pleasure of scalp gripping like earth. The sound of the reeds rushed through the window.

All the while the fish swam peacefully or darted into deeper, colder regions when she cast a line (not trying to hook it, but the arbitrary thought sharp on its own accord). In the morning she would hang laundry in the backyard sunlight and stop, feeling the sudden small departure; her hand might settle on her ribs, a drenched blouse would fall to the grass near her foot.

And then the night came when through the thick dream the fish rose squirming in the tunnel of her throat and sang, its mouth full of teeth like crooked gravestones, its song something she had never heard before. *Flying* was the lyric. The tremulous voice woke her, and she said Tell me *where* I am, tell me *where* I am, pressing down on the word as if to kill it. "You're here, you're here with me," William said. "It's all right, it's all right." And the fish then was gone again, slithering off down her throat, back to its home to rest up. She lay filled for hours then with a sense of the one who had made the untouchable fish with his own hands. And the words *Baby hush, hold the secret*—though she could not clearly remember his hands or the words. Only a distant darkness and the old weighted dreams of fingers pressing heavily down on her through those years when she had slept under a window—the violet neon sign of the bar across the street dusting her skin on the cot that didn't creak, a white, wooden washstand across the room with a mirror reflecting the moon. The moon itself a brittle, watchful face that didn't care, floating in the black sky, fat with light as if needing to be unplugged. *Baby now hush, hold the secret.*

"I dreamed a fish rose inside me and then the fish sang," she told William as he slept, wanting really to say, someone please, please help. Help me.

And so Sasha grew and ran through the blue house in underpants dabbled with miniature daisies or violets, a child one feels in the space behind the breastbone. Doris could only grit her teeth, leave rooms in which William chased the child through shadow and light, saying, I'm gonna get you, I'm gonna get you!—Sasha screaming in the fear of being caught—the high-pitched anticipatory squeal of what she wanted most.

Doris, trying to write a grocery list, instead wrote: "What I like is silence, order, and people who don't forget how to play the piano."

Sasha was unafraid. When she found a dead groundhog in the reeds, she picked it up in her arms and carried it into the kitchen, holding the still-warm body against her own, offering it to Doris as if it were cute and only sleeping. And Doris screamed, "Get out of my house! Get out of my house!" and Sasha ran off with the groundhog, shouting, "I'm sorry, I'm sorry." She returned later, flush faced, empty armed, and seemingly unhurt, her long hair curly and tangled. She trailed Doris with apologies, asking her why she was such a bad girl to bring the animal inside. Doris looked down and said, "The animal is dead, Sasha." Sasha looked up at her, unblinking, biting on the edge of her hand. "When you're dead you can't move or eat or dance or laugh. They put your body in a box and bury you in the ground and you never get to see the world again," she said, staring out the window. "And then even your body disappears."

Sasha, five minutes later, was dressed up in the aqua leotard and black velvet skirt; when she twirled, each pleat was a door opening to darkness. Doris watched from another room, sunlit. Sasha ran and fetched the tap shoes, black patent-leather with silver metal heels. She danced on the slate floor near the stove, the quick clicking sound that said she was getting good. "Come watch me, Mama!" the child called, and Doris entered the room to say, "My Sasha, you're really getting the hang of it, aren't you, honey?"—her voice swinging up and down in a search for warmth.

Doris painted a flower, and William said it was a wound and not to hang it.

....

Doris painted a building, and William said it was a man with no arms or legs and not to hang it.

And he begged her now to open at night, to speak with him, unclench the jaw, in short, *return*. Nothing is wrong, she said. Does nobody believe anymore in the inalienable rights of solitude? And the fish, smarter with age, found a way to feed; the emptiness inside of her grew. "I *said* nothing was wrong," she said, but she was alone in the house then, watering a plant.

And Sasha rode out through the field on her father's broad shoulders in the summer afternoons, down to the river where they'd sit and talk for hours. The child had dreams and stories that William returned with, the slightest stirring of wings filling his face, a certain quiver near the eyes and lips.

They begged her to join them in the beginning, but she'd say, "No, go on. Dirty rivers don't thrill me these days," and then laugh to cover herself, drawing it out like taut material that barely stretched.

And then they stopped asking.

To save something, a slice of herself, she came back to William at night, and he believed in her cries as cries of love. But she was flying herself like a kite in these sessions, giving herself entirely too much string. She would look down on herself, the stranger, and the strange man beside her. And her eyes watering until everything blurred.

She began to hate William then for believing her perfect lies, for not being smart enough to search out the fish when it wriggled behind her knees, those caves he kissed while she stood breaking. Hated him for strolling in his bones to the river with homemade rods, Sasha grown older now and walking beside him, a girl in red cut-off shorts with fringe tickling her thighs, her loose, buttery hair responding to the slightest breezes. And now she was telling William how she would grow up to be an astronaut, no matter *what*.

And like boys Doris remembered from school days, Sasha, trying to do homework at the kitchen table, would send her yellow pencils into the air, bring them back down again, clutching them. "There's little Martians in this rocket," she'd say, and Doris, turning from the sink, would say, "Are they nice Martians?" Then Sasha made the cat-eyed glasses out of cardboard, glued glitter on the outer edges, drew spaceships all over them with a black Flair. She began to wear them all the time, claimed she needed them to see. William loved this. "Artistic, just like her mother," he said. "She'll be the first astronaut who will know how to paint what she sees in the stars," he joked.

One winter night, Doris's mother called, a voice like a knife between the ribs, so smooth she didn't feel the hurt of it until the knife pulled out. Doris watched a soft snow fall beyond the window and listened. "What in the hell do you mean nothing is new? Everything in this world is new. There ought to be a law against newness. And each one of my children living far away on purpose. I want to know what's happening, how we've all ended up strangers, and why they're turning the country into a cartoon. Should a person become two-dimensional, or spectate?"

And her father got on the phone near the end of the rampage to say, "Don't worry, your mother's crazy. So how's life in the sticks?"

Then came a summer when she would sit on the peeling gray steps out back and wait for them to return from the river. And though she believed in no God that could listen or care, she prayed now, wholeheartedly, prayed to change, prayed to be happy and normal the way they imagined she was: a woman who took the time to give her chestnut hair a hundred strokes a night, who woke up and brightened her eyelids with green shadow that sparkled in the light so that the average

....

observer (which both William and Sasha had become) would look at her and think: pretty mother, pretty wife. Beautiful, really, and still young.

Sometimes when they came back they would hug her, Sasha around the waist, William the shoulders, their heads nuzzling, a revulsion spreading through her as she patted them and knew for the first time what the word *gingerly* meant, how ugly it was. The reeds glistened in the lilac light of August sunsets. Everything beautiful or good in the world was now a piercing reproach. The fish gained weight while Doris lost it, her clothes hanging loosely now, the bones showing through as if trying to make their point.

When Sasha turned eleven, William played records he'd inherited from his father, thick black plastic featuring the husky voice of Dietrich, a voice that Sasha learned to mimic. "Want to buy some illusions? Slightly used, secondhand?" And later, The Platters: "Oh yes, I'm the great pretender" (Sasha would sing this leaning on the piano while William played), "pretending that you're still around" (tinkling music in the pauses). And Doris stood in the doorway now, saying, "Really, you oughta take this show on the *road,*" chewing green gum, snapping it, trying to turn into another sort of woman altogether.

Later she would serve the dinner she cooked with the utmost care, setting the plates down for William and Sasha—they might have been on a date in a formal restaurant, facing each other across the small table, their silence deepening as she brought them their food. When she came back to the table with glasses of milk, she chewed her gum and looked down at them like a waitress in a diner. "Everything all right here?" she said, with a twang she meant to be humorous. They looked up at her in unison, wide-eyed.

When friends came to dinner one night, Sasha sat in the room, her presence like a song one knows is playing and cannot quite hear, the whole room seeming to listen to her though she said nothing and they chatted over their own strained listening. When finally she left the house, they all went to the window to see her running down the clay road in her brown dress with the cream-colored collar, her hair flying in the late light, running toward the dogs and Liam, the boy she thought she'd grow up and marry. He could juggle. He wore a faded blue jacket. They'd built a tree fort that looked out over the river. "Let's go down to the water!" they heard her cry. "Come on!" Finally, Doris, lingering behind the three of them at the window, said, "What are we doing? Come on, who needs a refill?"

And fixing the drinks in the kitchen, another window framed Sasha, the brown dress blowing like river water through her white legs, her arms outstretched like propellers twirling her down the clay road. Unswallowable was the grace and freedom in her changing, containing the brilliance of leaves that dangled, snow that wouldn't land, purple clover spreading, and, of course, the waves of summer. The child *belonged* to the year entirely, combining elements to lengthen it, herself a fifth season one watched, knowing there was no walking into it (the knowledge of those in hospital beds, turning to windows when visitors depart). How Sasha welcomed the curves, the hard budding, was seen in her face, anxiety laced with the flickerings of pride.

But Doris would sit up in the night and cry, "What? What is it? Do you need me?—a searchlight streaming from the girl's room down the hall. And William beside Doris, patient even when jarred from sleep, assured her she was only dreaming. How cruel the innately kind could be.

Red leaves clung to Sasha's hair and William always picked them out one at a time. And one day, walking, humming to herself under the backbend of a hard, gray sky, Doris saw a pile

....

of red leaves near the bottom of the hill and thought she might go fall in it, every cell in her body exhausted. But when she approached the pile, Liam and Sasha rose out of it—hatched—and though they'd simply been watching planes through the pile's dark spaces, imagining the complexity of the dashboard, the pilot's serious face peering down and seeing their huge pile as the tiniest drop of blood on the dead green ground, they blushed, seeing Doris. Liam ran off down the hill and Sasha looked at the ground and said, "Well hello, stranger, fancy meeting you here."

Later that evening Doris shocked herself, slapping Sasha's face. Her hand rose and covered her mouth while through sudden, blinding tears she watched Sasha scream, "I hate you! I despise you!"

William appeared in the doorway and said, "Would somebody please for Christ's sake tell me what's going on here?"

"She sassed me. And she's fooling around with the Sullivan boy," Doris said. "I'm sorry, I'm sorry I lost my temper." Then she ran from the house to stand on the back steps, catching her breath while William stayed behind to comfort the crying girl. Doris stood breathing and watching the yellow reeds bend in the moon. Then she moved to the window and saw the two of them seated on the couch, his arm slung around her, her face on his chest, William saying "She's only concerned about you. You don't yet know how boys can hurt. You have to start being *careful.*"

Doris drifted away from the window, past the reeds and down the sharp hill to the river, where she stood listening until she heard a bottle break against a rock and turned to see two boys, their faces blurry and white. "Smoke a joint?" one of them said, and the other said, "Oh *shit,* it's somebody's *mother!*" and they ran off, hooting.

She stood completely still, her arms crossed over her waist, the head that she carried so utterly straight now hanging down heavily, her eyes downstream on the dam where the river grew white and soft. Had she been conscious of these moments, they might have been a rare pleasure, so perfectly interested was she in the river. But it was the absence of consciousness that made this concentration possible. As soon as another bottle broke, this time on the far bank, she remembered herself, remembered all that went with being that self.

She walked back uphill to hide in the reeds until the lights in the house flicked off, each window now a dark square.

She walked down the hall and peered in on Sasha, who slept tangled in her sheets with one arm flung off the bed's edge where the moonlight streamed. Then down the hall and into the room where William, hearing her enter, said, "Hey, are you all right?"

"I think so. I just took a walk. I feel terrible."

"I guess this is the beginning of her growing pains," he said.

"I guess."

"Just try to remember when you were little," he said. "It's not easy."

"No, it's not," she said, and turned away from him on the far side of the bed. She closed her eyes.

"She'll be OK, though. We've done a good job."

"I need to sleep," Doris told him. "I'm really tired."

William's hand reached over and settled in the valley of her waist.

"I'm sorry," she said, "I need to sleep. I feel awful." And his hand lifted, the absence leaving a hole.

She could feel the fish as she fell asleep, slithering through her legs as she dropped into the dream, into the violet neon light of her childhood bedroom. She dreamed, *knowing* she was dreaming, until she saw herself as a child, small in the middle of the room, staring ahead at the washstand, the newly painted white wood of it, the mirror. Through the darkness bordering the dream, Doris walked slowly into the room of violet light as the adult she had become.

"Doris?" she said, and the child looked up at her, puzzled, then afraid. Dark wisps of hair framed the white face, the eyes too big. Doris asked the child, "Could you get me some water?" She watched the child turn slowly toward the sink, the dark braid a thick pendulum swinging as she walked, the night-gown, the nightgown, her favorite nightgown, her most despised nightgown, the map of the world all over it—the bright-colored countries surrounded by dark waters. He would point them out on her ribs, her thighs, trying not to tickle: *Turkey. Zimbabwe. Latvia. Greece.* And this is how they'd begin, her saying Really? Is it so far away that if I walked for a year I wouldn't be there? Him saying Baby you could walk for the rest of your life and never reach it.

How he knew everything! And she would say, "Where are we again?" *Turn over,* he'd say, Turn over, and then his hand on the lowest part of her spine pressed down and he said, We're here, baby, we're right here, and she would cry.

And now Doris watched the child bring the water toward her, the heavy eyes dark and downcast in shyness and shame, her feet small and prehensile on the bare wooden floor where the violet neon lay.

The little girl outstretched her arm, extending the water in the clearest of glasses. The water slid to a stop. The child's eyes looked up angry, betrayed, enormously sad, so that Doris, trapped in the dream's silence, ached for words to say I'm sorry. I'm sorry I left you, I'm sorry I went away. I had no choice.

Instead, she took the glass of water, the child watching while she began to drink, while squirming and expanding in the space between her ribs came the fish, rising into her breast and then her throat, the child backing away and the nightgown beginning to vanish one continent at a time, leaving the child naked, her narrow shoulders hunching inward, and then she was gone. The emptied room with the white washstand and the violet light grew utterly clear, enlarged, then vanished, the dreamer gone too, and the fish filling her mind so entirely that her own face was fish. She woke like that, silvery and cold, her legs closed tightly as if to become one, her arms pinioned to her side and melting inward, mouth jarred open and tasting of blood and salt, one unblinking eye fixed on William, waiting in the dark dryness of clean white sheets for him to wake and tell her where she was, and was she dreaming.

By the Light of Friendship

....

➤ Through salt air Sam Taren walked toward the bus stop where a green wooden enclosure sheltered two women. One held a white stray cat on her broad lap, the other was smoking. Long red nails dragged through the dirty white fur; the cat purred loudly.

"It's too damn hot to hold a cat like that, Gina," said the smoker, and then, seeing Sam approach, said, "Look, a dead man."

It was true that he was very pale and moved slowly now through the heat, but that was only a terrible hangover that he hadn't been able to cure despite a day of naps and orange juice and sitting by the fan with his eyes closed listening to people walk past his window up the sandy road toward the ocean.

"Evening," he said to the two at the bus stop.

"Hello," they barely murmured together. The cat languidly lifted its head and squinted at him.

"Waiting on the Portland bus?" he asked them, to make sure he was in the right place, and they nodded their heads. They were both close to fifty, he gathered. The one with the cat had given herself an orange tan from a bottle. His mother had done that every year. He felt a vague anxiety in his stomach, like a small amount of spoiled food. He looked at the dark line ending on the woman's jaw, how white her neck suddenly was, and then, without planning on it, said, "I'm a little nervous tonight."

"You look like you need to sleep for about a year and a half, no offense," said the smoker, whose name was Lois. She was a stocky, freckled woman who looked like she could sit in a bar and tell a good joke. Around her neck she wore a string of orange coral.

"That bad?" Sam said. "Maybe it's just because I'm nervous." He'd repeated this in hopes that they'd pursue it, and they did.

"Oh yeah?" said Lois. "Why?" He saw her nudge the one with the cat, who nudged her back harder. Like schoolgirls, he thought.

"My daughter's coming in on that bus. I haven't seen her in three years."

He saw the women look at each other.

"Three years," said Lois. She blew a chain of smoke rings, one for each year, and he watched them ride out into the humid evening air.

"That's a long time," Gina said, and crossed her orange arms. The undersides were milk white, with freckles. Now Lois moved away from Gina and motioned with her hand to Sam. "Sit down between us if you'd like." Her voice had an edge of sarcasm, but Sam was comfortable here; he felt superior to these women, as he always did with women for whom he felt not even a flickering of desire.

He sat down between them and crossed his arms and leaned his head back on the green wooden wall behind him, closing his eyes. He wanted this whole visit to be over with before it had even begun.

"If you don't mind me asking, why has it been three years?" Lois said. Sam opened his eyes and watched an old man shuffle by in slippers and a baseball cap, talking to himself.

"It's a long story. You know, divorce, bad times. . . ."

"Oh yes," Lois said, "We know." And the two women burst out laughing for a split second: Ha!—then fell silent just as quickly.

"It's not easy," Gina said, like an apology for their laughter. "It sure can be hell."

Lois said, "You can always get yourself a friend and go out every night and sit together in the Acme parking lot drinking Colt 45 and listening to what the deejay calls music you fell in love by. See the pyramids along the Nile." Lois began to sing that old song. She had an undeniably terrible voice.

Gina laughed, then looked embarrassed for a moment and fixed her hair with her hands. "Lois is in rare form tonight," she said.

"Oh heck," Sam said (he almost never said "heck," and listening to himself say it now further depressed him), "sounds good to me. I could go for a Colt right now, and if we weren't waiting I'd invite you both to my bar. We could tie one on and watch the Phillies get whipped." As the words left his lips, Sam remembered that he'd decided to quit drinking this morning when he'd opened his eyes to the bright, desolate sunlight. A dark space opened up within him now.

"You have a bar?" Gina said. She leaned forward and turned to look at him, eyebrows raised.

"No, no, I just mean the bar I drink at lately. It's on the boardwalk. You know Tommy's Place?"

"We know it," Lois said. "All that taxidermy shit turns my stomach."

Sam smiled. His own stomach tightened. Soon his daughter would step down off the bus. As hard as he tried, he could not remember exactly what she looked like, much less how she might have changed. He was afraid of trying to imagine the expression of her eyes.

"So here we are, waiting on Gina's sick mother and a little girl you haven't seen in three years," Lois said.

"Actually it's almost been three and a half," Sam said. He was not conscious of wanting to be challenged, or accused, but felt disappointed when both women were quiet after this admission.

"So how old is she?" Gina finally said.

"She'd be fourteen by now."

"How long's she staying?" Gina said.

"One week."

Lois started laughing. "Well, you're in for an education, bless your heart. A fourteen-year-old girl!" She clapped her hands twice. "I have one of my own." With her finger Lois drew several quick loops in the air next to her head and said the word *koo-koo*. "You oughta call me up and I'll put Rochelle on the phone and the two of them can make plans to grease up with coconut oil then walk the beach together rolling their eyes and saying, 'Oh my God!' That's about all they do at that age, ya know."

Sam held his eyes wide open now. The sky above the squat line of buildings across the street was a vibrant purple, autumnal somehow. He squinted at the bright moon and tried hard to picture his daughter, but the only image his mind would hold was how she looked on Halloween one year, a seven-year-old nurse who'd taken it upon herself to transform her new red school shoes with white house paint. Sam had exploded with rage and made her stay inside for Halloween as a punishment, and now the memory of her face that night was something he returned to almost every day, obsessively.

Lois was telling a story.

". . . and so Rochelle looks at me wide-eyed and says no, nobody's here, but I have enough mother instinct to know it's a lie, so I start walking around the room. First I find the mayonnaise jar filled with vodka under her pillow. Then I open the closet and there's the Mulveen boy, crouched under her dresses like he's in heat. Mulveen, I said, should I boot your ass out of here, or will you leave like a human being?"

Sam suddenly stood up and announced that he was going across the street to buy a can of beer or two. He knew that in a while his nerves would be shot without it. His legs felt weak as he walked.

He returned with a beer for each of them and took his seat again. The darkening air seemed to have come forward like water into the wooden enclosure, and now Gina was speaking of her mother's illness. "I don't see why I have to tell her the whole truth. She's seventy years old. Why should her last days be spent worrying about how many cells were eaten up that day?"

"Well, whatever Gina, but I think a person has a right to know when they're checking out."

They fell silent, sipped their beers and watched the bright stars for a while. Sam began to feel strangely protected in their presence. A part of him wished the bus would be hours late so the three of them could sit and watch the stars and moon in the purple sky and knock back some cold beers. They could talk and he could listen. He would revel in the safety of how little whatever transpired here could matter.

When Gina shifted, then got up to stretch, setting the cat down on the sidewalk, Sam wanted to pull her back to her seat. As she stretched he watched her shirt rise and reveal a doughy, white stomach. She was a tall, large-boned woman with a long, graceful neck. After stretching, she did just what Sam wanted her to, she scooped the cat up and sat back down, this time even closer to Sam. He could feel the warmth of her body. She began stroking the cat again and humming what sounded like "Mame."

"If the bus doesn't come in the next ten minutes I'm calling Greyhound," Lois said.

·······································

"Lois love, they're always late, just enjoy the evening," Gina said.

But a minute later the bus was coming. The headlights were two blind eyes of a creature Sam wanted to run from. He sprung to his feet, cleared his throat, and now stood staring at the lights getting closer, as if the pain this caused his eyes could distract him, calm him, or maybe punish him. His heart pounded violently. He would embrace her, like fathers on TV commercials. "Well hey, kiddo," he'd rehearsed by the mirror. He would carry her suitcase, which she said would be yellow: "You'll know it's me when you see a blonde girl in blue glasses who needs to go on a major diet. And I'll carry this small yellow suitcase you might even remember, considering you bought it," she'd written. She'd signed the card: "Rettie (Loretta) Taren."

The bus had stopped, the doors were yanked open, and the first to disembark was a mother and her three small children. Next came a large nun. Next a man in an undershirt. Sam stared at each person as if there was a small chance that she might be Loretta. On his face he held a stiff smile that even a stranger could see was pained. His heart slammed inside of him while a voice in his head seemed to be screaming "Hi! I am so glad you came!"

Gina's mother stepped down. She had a regal presence; her hair was dyed red, her chin was lifted high, she wore pearls and a simple navy blue dress. Sam was vaguely aware of Gina and Lois welcoming her beside him. Next to step off the bus was a young boy carrying a huge suitcase with a rope tied to the handle; the boy pulled the suitcase down the sidewalk like a stubborn black dog, cursing it. Several lone, exhausted-looking adults filed off, and then there was nobody.

She's hiding in the back of the bus, Sam thought. She's as nervous as me. The thought gave him courage and filled him with affection. The bus driver looked at him, then back down at whatever he was doodling on.

"Loretta?" Sam called down the dark aisle. "Loretta Taren? I mean, Rettie?"

The bus driver turned around. "Sir?" he said. "You the one waiting on your daughter?"

"That would be me," Sam said. Terrible visions crowded into his mind; she had been killed at one of the rest stops. She'd choked to death on the bus, and they'd had to let her off somewhere in North Jersey. He had not felt the deep terror of parenthood in so long; now he almost was sick with it.

The bus driver was staring at him.

"What is it?" Sam snapped.

"Here's a note for you. The girl made me promise to give it to you. Such a sweet girl, I said yes. Usually I wouldn't make a point of playing postman."

The bus driver pulled an envelope from his jacket pocket and handed it to Sam.

"Thank you, thanks a lot," Sam said, and felt the bus driver's silence as a judgment. He stepped down off the bus. The air smelled saltier, seemed darker.

"Sam!" It was Gina's voice. They stood on the other side of the street. "Come meet my mother!" Gina called. "Bring your girl!"

He crossed the street. He held the envelope tightly in his sweaty hand.

"Where is she?" they asked. He opened the envelope; it was as if opening it in public could deprive it of what he feared would be its intense privacy. And yet, when he read it and found nothing of the sort, his heart sank. The note was on a piece of stationery with flowers all over it and said simply that she'd decided this wasn't quite the time to visit after all, but maybe another time. He wasn't prepared to feel the profound sadness that overtook him now.

The three women looked at him. "Well?"

"She's not feeling well so she couldn't come."

....

"Too bad! Really too bad! Well, anyhow, this is my mother, Julia Vincenti. And this is Sam, Mother."

The woman extended her hand and said, "Sam, how do you do?"

"Nice to meet you," Sam said. "Hope to see you all again sometime." He turned to walk away.

"Oh no you don't," Lois said. Sam stopped and looked back at her.

"Why don't you come out with us? Come back to the house first, and then we'll go somewhere. Don't be disappointed all by yourself!"

He shrugged, then found himself walking beside them, but the intimacy he'd felt at the bus stop had been lost, punctured by Loretta's letter and dispersed into the night air. Gina was whistling quietly; again it sounded like "Mame." Was that the only song she knew? Lois was telling her mother about the kids, how they were excited she was coming. Sam saw Gina and Lois trade looks every so often. It was as if they used their eyes to anchor each other. And each glance exchanged meant something that only the two women knew.

He stood on the dark front porch by the lit doorway of the old beach house while the children—there must've been a dozen of them, all sunburned and white-teethed with shrill voices, some grown with babies—greeted their grandmother. They had made her dinner; Sam could see it waiting on the white table, steaming asparagus, corn, and steak. Bold flowers sat in a blue vase on the table's center.

Finally Lois turned around and said, "Sam, come on in. It'll be a while. Gina and I need to wash up and make sure everything's settled here. Take a seat, watch TV, relax."

He took a seat and watched the television, but did not relax. One of the older granddaughters offered him a seat at the table, but he refused. The voices on the television began to blend with the voices at the table. What am I doing here? he wondered.

He felt unable to look away from the television. Every so often Lois or Gina stood before him with a bowl of Spanish peanuts, saying, "Have some. It won't be long now before we can go out, Sammy." Somehow both of them had started calling him "Sammy" as soon as he'd stepped in the house.

"So what kind of music do you like, Sammy?"

They were driving now, the three of them, Sam in the back seat and Lois at the wheel. The old paneled station wagon had a peculiar smell to it, something too hard to pin down, like the smell of someone else's entire history.

"I like Engelbert Humperdinck," Sam said. It was a lie—he'd just felt like saying the name. His wife had liked him, but not even that much. Once she'd thumbtacked his album cover onto the bathroom wall.

"Engelbert Humperdinck," Lois said. "I can't say Engelbert ever rang my chimes."

"You don't have any chimes," Gina said.

"What?"

"Never mind."

They sailed down a small, dark highway, the marshland on either side of them spread out for miles, the air thick with the smell of fish. Lois turned on the radio. Each of them sipped on a cold beer. Sam was beginning to relax and felt safe knowing the cooler behind him was full. This was the deepest pleasure he knew, this cold beer pouring into him on a summer night; for a few moments he gave himself to the sensuality of it and sang along with the song on the radio.

"So how do you two know each other, anyway?" he said. They looked at each other and laughed. "You tell it," Lois said.

"I'm not in the mood. I told it last time."

....

"Oh, come on. No? Well then, I'll tell it," Lois said. "We've known each other now for forty-six years. We met as third graders at Immaculate Conception School in Philadelphia. Gina was the brain who won the spelling bees, I was the fat kid whose knee socks were always down around the ankles. The nuns liked to beat the hell out of me. Then, by sixth grade, Gina was an odd giraffe who sucked on her hair all day, and I was slimmed down and thought I was Betty Grable, but we were suddenly best friends. Blood sisters."

Sam smiled, but an image of Loretta filled his mind and merged with a friend from his childhood, a boy standing in a sandlot near a fence.

"Anyhow, somehow we made it through high school, though Lois got suspended fourteen thousand times," Gina said, apparently taking over now.

"You were no angel either, honey," Lois said.

"Tell him about the time we lined the statues of the saints up at the men's urinals," Gina said. She was loosened by the beer, and her voice was getting steadily louder.

"Oh hell," Lois said, and looked at Sam in the rear-view. But now she was laughing—both of them were. "God, I haven't thought of that in ten years!" Lois cried. "Why do you do this to me?"

A silence fell, and Sam watched Gina's profile in the dark; she was turned toward Lois, watching her.

"You lined the saints up at the urinals?" he said now, smiling, taking refuge in the image. "You actually lined the saints up at the urinals?"

"Hell yes," Gina said. "Course it was Lois's idea. You should've seen how patient all those saints looked waiting in line."

"Not all of them. Don't you remember Connie Delilio saying Saint Benedict looked like he couldn't hold it?"

"Connie Delilio!"

"She's dead."

"Poor soul."

"Anyhow," Lois started up again, "after the days of saints and urinals, we got ourselves married—Gina first, and then me." She was pulling the car into a large, empty parking lot. At the edge of the lot tall reeds were bending in the sea breeze.

"There's a pavilion where we can sit, Sammy. You can see all the lights in Wildwood, and it's right out over the ocean. Better than air-conditioning."

In the pavilion they set the cooler on one bench, then the three of them took a seat on the bench closest to the sea, which pounded and crashed underneath them. It looked so black and white under the moon. Sam didn't look at the ocean very often. He wasn't drawn to its mystery or power. It frightened him to stare at it for too long. He looked off to the left, toward the long string of neon lights in Wildwood.

"Isn't it heaven up here? So where was I?" Lois said. "So I get pregnant, then Gina follows suit, and we end up living right down the street from each other in a hellhole called Cabrini Heights. Then we each have four more babies, right in a row, the way all good Catholic girls did back then. You see, Sammy, we were fools in love with the pope."

"You were in love with him, Lois, I was only afraid of him."

"Remember Father Monegal, that afternoon we went to see him together?" Lois said, turning to Gina, who laughed and said, "No, don't remind me."

It seemed both women were on the edge of an odd hilarity tonight. Sam was beginning to feel like an intruder. The more they spoke of their past together, the more solitary he felt. And yet he loved a story. He loved listening to the reasons that people's lives became entwined.

"So what was this Father Monegal all about?" he ventured.

"'Child of God, let me make this crystal clear to you!'" Gina boomed in an Irish accent. All her reticence was gone; appar-

....
ently she'd done a perfect imitation because Lois was laughing and clapping.

"'Child of God, a woman's blessed job is to bear fruit.'"

"He used to close his eyes when he spoke to you, and he always grabbed your wrist with his clammy hand."

"He was a little crazy and didn't understand a thing about why a woman might not want to be a baby machine, but he was kind. He visited my Jimmy in the hospital and stayed into the night when we thought we were losing him. Gave him last rites and all."

"What a time that was," Gina said. "Good God."

"Is Father Monegal still alive?" Sam said. He was sipping on another beer and staring out at the black horizon.

"He died years ago," Lois said. "I'll never forget him, though."

"Who could forget?"

"When Bill left me, he played Santa Claus for the kids that year. I mean he bought the whole shebang—each kid got three or four toys, more than they got when Bill was there! And Gina stayed up with me all night and put all the damn toys together, didn't ya, babe?"

Gina laughed. "Did I have a choice?"

"Bill your husband?" Sam said.

"That's right. Old Bill was my husband. Mr. Red Bull Inn Bill."

Gina laughed at this private joke, then said, "Lois, don't go off on a Bill tangent, please. Not here in front of the ocean." Gina was standing up now, leaning out into the spray. Sam looked at her long legs. They seemed too bare up here.

"If you think about it, you'd realize I haven't gone on a Bill tangent for over a year, Gina."

Now they were all quiet. Finally, Sam, uncomfortable and lonely in the prolonged silence, said, "So you two have really been friends for forty-six years?"

"That's right. And I wouldn't have survived this life without her." That was Lois.

Gina turned back to them and smiled. Wind whipped through her hair and shirt. She looked young, tall, and full of energy.

"You would've survived, but you wouldn't have had half as much fun," she said. Her voice cracked and quivered, like the voice of someone about to cry.

"What's wrong, honey?" Lois said. "Come here, sit down."

Gina came and sat down beside her, her arms folded. Now on the bench there was a big gap between Sam and the two women.

"What is it?" Lois said, softly.

"I don't know," Gina cried.

"Is it your mother?"

"No. Yes, it's everything," Gina said, and her friend moved over and held her. Gina's sobs were deep; her body shook.

Sam headed quietly out of the pavilion and into the moonlit lot. He felt lonelier than he had in a long time. He looked at the car and decided against sitting in it. He walked down under the pavilion, where he could barely hear Gina's sobbing, and where the tide was rising, darkening the cool sand.

"Sam?" the two voices called out. "Where are you?"

They waited a moment when he didn't answer, and again called, "Sam? Where are you?"

It was like hiding in a game. He would baffle them. He would make them search for a while.

"Where the hell is he?" Lois said.

He heard their footsteps above his head, stomping down the boards of the pavilion. He could look up like a child through the cracks and see their shoes, their legs.

Now they were out in the parking lot. Sam's heart was beating hard; his throat was filled as if he was just about to call out their names. He took a sip of his beer.

"Sam! Damn it, where the hell did you go?"

They looked in the car; when they opened the doors, the interior light lit them up.

"Not in here," Lois said. "But then where?"

There was something painfully familiar about all this, Sam thought, as gradually he remembered he had done this as a child when he'd lived for a while with an aunt and uncle. He'd hid behind their hedges one spring night, as a joke, and it had taken them a long time to realize he was missing. When they did, they were frantic with worry. He hadn't been much older than five or six. The two of them, both tall and skinny, and a neighbor woman who had the habit of pinching him, had stood on the porch, just inches away from where he hid, talking about what a spoiled child he was, how willful, how hard to like, how relieved they would be when he could go live with his parents again.

It had shocked him, and he had cried and bit into his fist. "If I were you, I'd give him a good beating when he gets in," the neighbor woman had said.

Sam felt embarrassed by the memory and let it be replaced by the sadness over his daughter's visit. But there was a bigger sadness here that he couldn't name. Now he ducked out from underneath the pavilion and walked toward the lot, where Lois and Gina were waiting in the front seat. His face burned with shame against the salt air.

He opened the back door. "I just took a little walk," he told them. "Thought I'd give you some privacy."

"No problem," Lois said.

They drove back to town in silence. Sam wanted to break the silence, wanted to say something profound, but he didn't know what. "Ah, life," he tried, but neither woman responded. He stared out the window at the night sky, and they dropped him off at his apartment.

"Have a good night, now," they told him, and he was surprised when they didn't say anything at all about keeping in touch. He felt hurt by it, and foolish for feeling that way. Who were they, anyhow?

In the doorway of his bedroom, he flicked on the lights. He had planned on sleeping on the couch tonight, planned on giving this room to Loretta, whoever she was. He looked at the bed—new, white sheets trimmed with blue butterflies. He had folded them down diagonally, as his wife had done early in their marriage. On the dresser were white roses in a blue vase that said "Ocean City." The room was immaculate for the first time since he had lived there.

He turned off the light and walked into the hall, thinking now of Gina and Lois sitting up late on their front porch, talking quietly, one of their grandchildren coming out in pajamas to have a bad dream soothed away. Gina would lift the child onto her lap. Lois would tell the child a story, something funny from her own childhood, and gradually the child's tears would change to laughter. Then sleep would come. Sam could see Gina carrying the child back to his bed, how for one second in the moonlight the eyes of the child would open wide, then close.

But now the child was clearly Loretta, a baby, and it was himself carrying her down the dim hall, himself as a young man, a boy really, in love with that tiny life in his arms. He ached now to hold that baby again, to be that young man who had told his wife, "I'd die for this child in a second. I never thought I would love her this much."

Sam stripped and got into the bed. What happened to me, said a voice that was not his own, a voice in the far corner of his mind. My life. His hand rested heavily on his pounding heart. A strong breeze came into the room and washed over him in the bed.

Then he was out of bed, crouched on the floor, holding his face in his hands, and for a moment thought he would cry, really cry, but did not. He was not sure he knew how to cry. He remembered the sound of Gina's crying at the ocean. She is what I'd sound like, he thought, if I could cry. If I could cry, I would sound like her.

He stayed in that position for a long time, listening.

Director of the World

··

➢ You can pretend when your father comes home from the war he's all right, same as he'll pretend same as your mother will pretend. First, the big supper!

She got in her apron, wore it like the miniskirt, tied the sash tight, put on nylons, high heels, nothing else, just the apron with the fruit that's the wrong color meaning oranges are grape and vice versa, someone's humor we don't need it.

He's with his keys, we don't know what they go to, there are fifty-two of them altogether, only I know because only I counted, it was night, they were over my head. All he wanted to do was cry, that was how it had to be. He said to her, you get out of bed so I can cry in peace. Get out of my dream. Out! Really loud, you would think to yourself, the neighbors.

Right over my head so on the gray couch looking at the ceiling I thought they might crash on through, would they be bare, I wouldn't want to see, I'm not like the others, especially the ones who do it, and they do it in the outdoors, for instance in a parking lot, even though I would say, "There's broken glass and you'll get cut." Once a girl said she likes it, the getting cut part, by the name of Yolanda Finch, not a lie.

You can still be a child, for instance, you can say no, I don't think I'll grow up yet, then you think it so hard, it works, and you go to a movie and get the child rate maybe all your life hunching.

JANE McCAFFERTY

And sometimes you can feel like saying to your mother that you don't like the world, so this way she'll say drink some milk, take a nap, or make a joke and say the world don't like you either but don't you already know that.

In the mornings you all sit at the white table, the kitchen seems full of fog, there should be a horn, she looks all right in her nightgown, he wears his underwear, calls them *drawers* and maybe his shoes on too, maybe even combat boots depending on his mood, you think to yourself I'm not inviting friends over anymore and your mother makes the joke, What friends?

There are all those times when you forget who you are. It can be like you're the impersonator and they're paying you, you can convince so many that you are yourself.

So she's standing at the stove frying eggs which he loves so we think, when all the sudden he says "Tell me why you're cooking eggs." She turns around and says, For breakfast Silly, smiling but it's the crying tone now.

Also outside there is yelling. The bottle breaker likes the morning and to say Somebody Somebody. Like a rooster it could wake you, we're not on a farm, you can go to the windows press your forehead and see the bottles breaking. You might want to go to a farm for health, a little air. I could grow up and have a farmhouse, very quiet, I love nature and wouldn't need a car.

After he said "Breakfast, is that right?" he took the ring of fifty-two keys and examined it like a huge seaweed thing, it should be dripping wet. He shook it just a little, a little music in the kitchen, there goes the hole.

Important, he said. Important thing is to be a good *spy*. My mother turned around and said Come again?

Zenia, he said to me, Sometimes I look at you and think you're less than human. And I mean that as a compliment.

And my mother turned from the stove. Very lonely when she said nothing, and I said Why you got that look, it's a joke, he's funny, he's making a joke. Why are you looking so serious, spoiling everything! My father nods, then gives me the wink. Then says in the old voice: First we need raincoats.

That's right, I said, and then we laugh, do we know where we are? The nervous laughter, all those keys!

"Good-bye," I said to her. She folded her thin arms, that's all I can say, I wasn't interested in her eyes.

So we got into his car, which first he stood back, looked at smiling. This piece of shit, he said, it'll take us nowhere fast.

We got into the front seat, red like blood under my legs. Sun washed through the windshield so we squinted. I just clearly saw how I was, another person, and quiet in the piece of shit car.

We didn't look at each other, how could we. How do you say why you don't look. To get through it you stare straight ahead.

You miss me? How much? As much as you thought? and he asked me all three questions as usual before I even answered the first.

What did I say? Nothing! I loved him! I should've found my voice!

He started up the car, I was all right in his book he said. We drove, there was that sizzling sound, so the streets were wet. Tulip tree, he said, every time we passed one. And made an explosion sound. The trees were beautiful.

"Where's the raincoat store, honey?" he said, then looked over. I saw his eyes, you don't know how a hand can reach out of the pupil, which in him was then large, but I saw the hand reaching, maybe waving good-bye, maybe I wanted to say that too, good-bye! But you just look at each other anyway, it's a part of your life, your life and not to block things out.

"I don't know any raincoat stores," I said, talking in the tone of everything's fine. "Raincoat stores, hmmmm," I said, very cheerful since the silence. Then I said, "Can we turn on the radio?" and he said, "Radio?" and got a big smile on his face. "That's a fantastic idea!"

You thought I invented the radio!

When really, when I was small, it was us on the road listening to the radio, all the windows rolled down, that's how the years went by I think now, and then I was very happy. You can't imagine how many good songs there were. Every so often his hand reaching over and sitting on my head like a nice cap to keep my thoughts down.

You think about the hands you held once.

We sailed down the freeway like a speedboat. I could see the road was water going fast. He said, "Sears," and I nodded, very cheerful. There was green sky out the windows, and he had his keys on his lap like a small dog, that was the sad part. His hand smoothing them.

Before Sears there was a bar. I forget the name. The bartender told him No little girls and he said Little? Who's little? Then he said, Please, if she sits quiet on the end stool? The bartender shrugged. My father said he just wanted one drink and he'd be mighty quick.

He made it so quick my eyes didn't even get used to the dark. I was still blind from the daylight shining off the wet gray sidewalk. He put his finger up in the air and said, "To the raincoats!"

You can pretend people aren't gone, but really they are, that doesn't mean they're not them anymore. They're still blood.

In Sears he said for instance, "No we don't need any help" to the saleslady, and he said it so quiet, like a whisper, and his eyes fluttered, fluttered, froze.

He took us to the boy section. Girl raincoats aren't for spies, he said.

He picked out one real nice spy raincoat, size twelve, beige colored plain, dark lining.

Try it on, Zeen Queen.

That was the old name. It will tell you he had a sense of humor, also he made up songs for me and sang them when we drove. "Zeen-Queen, Zeen-Queen, what did the world mean."

In the spy coat I stood before the mirror and he gave a whistle. You know the whole Sears heard. "Beautiful!" he said, and asked a stranger, "Whatta you think, does she look like a spy?"

The stranger nodded very cheerful. Then we went to the men's section. He found a raincoat just like mine, three times as big and put it on. Handsome. I'm telling you.

He looked in the mirror, not at the front self but walking away he looked at the back of him, looking over his shoulder to see how he looked leaving.

"We're all set," he said.

"Sure Papa, what you say goes."

And then I snap my finger like the Three Stooges on the television, he used to watch with me on his shoulders. He used to be like that, a man watching television with a girl on his shoulders, four years old and smaller, before he saw them stick grenades up the village girls which he told us in his old voice in the other bar where the bartender didn't care how long I stayed. That was later in the night. We were in our spy coats. Let me go backwards.

He said at least he wasn't a Seal. They do things he couldn't imagine. The hardest things, he said. And black seals were slipping all over inside my head throwing red balls so when I told him, he had to say, "Not those kind of seals! Christ!" I was then blocking it out and seeing his hand on the pile of keys making him popular in the bar. They kept saying "Why all the keys? Why all the keys?" Laughing together against him.

There are so many people think it's a joke. Pick up your keys, we can leave the bar, I told him.

We were then back in the car. We drove in the dark playing spies. "There is so much to spy on," he kept saying. Beeped the horn. There in the Valiant the red front seat with the moon. It's dark enough. Both of us in our spy coats, he slides through the rich section, where I know people for instance from school. They look like magazines, very rich. He slid by in the car and we stared very hard at the houses. We spied on many things, the lit windows, the yellow flowers, the big lawns, we saw it all. A sprinkler, a sprinkler, shooting the air. An old man looking at the sky with a dog in his arms.

Then we spied on other things. The highway. We stared very hard at the other cars when they drove by us. Spying right on the driver, if they saw we didn't look away, kept spying.

Soon we were going so slow. We had a lane to ourself. Twenty miles an hour right on the freeway. He said he didn't care where his ass ended up. I remember his tone. We drove along.

"We could go spy on Supermarket," he said, he forgot the name. We did that, we drove slow by the window of Shop N' Save, all lit up and the shoppers inside with carts not knowing we were spying, and then he turned into the director.

"Keep shopping," he told them, don't stop. He nodded, he told them they were doing a good job. He was the director now. We were back on the freeway and he told the cars, "That's right, keep it up now, keep driving, that's right," and he nodded. He told them he was very proud of them, and also the light, he told it to change red so we could stop, then told the light it was very good, he was proud. We then passed a woman lit up in a glass telephone booth. "Insert the coin and make the call," he directed, and she did.

Also we went to the factory, leather I think, the one under

the bridge, there was a big chain link fence, we spied through it, we saw the factory wall. Our shadows were there. How his hands were on the fence is very clear. He shook the fence. Then he put the collar of his spy coat up and told me to do the same. We looked at our black shadows on the wall and waved to them. Then, back to the car, and now the keys between us and also his hand patting them. Next.

We spied on sheep. They are downstate, way past Dover. We were flying, he directed the other cars, "Keep going, you're all doing fine, just keep driving." He directed the moon, he said, "Shine shine and don't fall down," and to the litter he pointed and said "Lie there and look awful" and we were going so fast the farmhouses float, float up off the land, he told them to. All the land was black and under the sheep. He pulled the car up and shined his lights on the sheep. We spied very long, he told them they were being good, doing a good job. He said stand there and look at us and they did. White wool bodies, black faces, pink ears and black legs. When they spoke the sound was men trapped inside.

Look at these poor animals, he said, they don't want to be here, they want to go to another planet, can't you tell? I kept looking at the sheep, just looking now, not spying. And they turned their faces, you could see the world turning away from you.

All the sheep were walking away and then he said "Your mother's in a dream world, a dream world all her own, and I don't know what's happening here." You kissed him as he cried like kissing him good-bye and hello at the same time you're not sure, push him away as hard as you can.

Very quiet. Back upstate. We drove and drove. Then we went down our street. It is very narrow, it never struck me how narrow our street was but then it did, that night, all the houses stuck together, we got claustrophobia. But he told the houses

"Keep standing still in the moonlight." And then he parked right outside our house.

We spied from the car. Tears were running down. Already she was in the nightgown, roses on white. First she was in one window, her arms crossed. "You just stand there with your arms crossed," he said. "That's right. Then in another window. That's right," he said. "Walk from window to window in your roses." She then stood in the big window, lit a cigarette as he told her, "Light a cigarette. Now inhale. That's good, now smoke it." She smoked it, and he said "Perfect."

Let's go in please.

In the morning I woke up, he was gone. I could feel it, it's for good, maybe he went to another country. You don't hope for return.

My mother cried and didn't get dressed for some time. Then a new man came, one who brought me presents:

1 crossword books
2 red socks with light blue stars
3 underwater snow scene thing
4 china mouse with gray vest plus spectacles
5 poster of sea gull flying over ocean
6 notebook, pencils
7 a record by a fellow named B. B. King
8 several times, candy, including Baby Ruth, a personal
  favorite

A *very* nice man, nobody should complain, by the name of Everett and feels great sympathy for all the peoples of the earth. He and my mother sit at the white table now, two voices behind the wall, you can get the glass and press your ear. She said to him last night I'm like my father, and she can't help that damn it. Other people's husbands come back just fine, she said, in a way I'm glad he's gone. It's a big relief, she said. They were drinking hot water with lemon in it like they do with saltines.

To peel off my black leotards every night then to sleep, not under the blankets, they itch my skin, but under his spy coat, it smells like him, left behind on purpose, don't you think? and I clench my eyes shut and there is the sheep, every time, rising off the black land into the stars and inside the sheep's mind me pushing him away and his voice so clear in my head still direct-ing. He tells the sheep *Fly* and they're already flying, so they fly.

Good-bye Now

....

➤ Their ease astonished the girl, Sonja, especially her own brother's voice and the way he held his body, as if it were a prize someone would receive someday, but not yet. His arms were crossed, his head cocked back, his shoulders had broadened as if to contain the unspeakable knowledge he breathed in like air. His name was John and he was talking now—his voice no longer cracked with change—and in the eyes of the other boys respect and envy mingled, making each one seem more solitary. He was telling them of an abandoned building he'd discovered downtown the day before with Reno, who was presently grounded. Reno was John's sidekick, a wild-eyed boy who never spoke much but was rumored to have had sex behind Jimmy's Steakhouse with Theresa, a girl from Browntown whose mother made her scrub the sidewalk every day and whom Reno loved. Nobody had seen the girl, but she was somehow always present. Even when Reno wasn't with them the fact of what he'd done with the girl was a spirit they held inside of them—for Sonja the spirit of awe that Reno and the girl had been so in love they'd had no choice, they couldn't control themselves. Sonja had ridden her bike up to the small field behind Jimmy's just to see the place where they'd been, the grass and weeds bordered by railroad tracks and the smell of fries and meat bending in the air like an enclosure. She'd gone there just after dusk, alone, and the place had seemed more sacred than profane, even as her face burned breathing in the spirit of so much contagious intimacy. She was young enough to believe Reno and the girl were no longer lonely because of what they'd done, and it was this imagined end to loneliness that drew her in. What impressed her most was the desperation she believed had to rise to the surface before loneliness could be given to another. Riding away from the site that night, down the smooth, gray roads in the dark, she looked toward the lit windows of other houses as if there might be a face framed in one of them looking for her.

But now they were all on the corner of Ash Road under an autumn sky so blue and low, so cloudless, that even the most oblivious of them held a vague awareness of the light's clarity, the sun's new distance. The memory of summer was like a small grief that continued to bond them—they'd been a pack of wild banshees, as their mothers said, running holy terrors through the streets and alleys and yards all day and night until they fell into beds and slept almost instantly, anxieties squelched by physical exertion and by the certainty that tomorrow bright sun would blast through their windows and onto their beds before the others gathered on the ground below to holler up, "Yo, wake up ya sad sack of dog crap!" or "Hey weenie brain, come play ball!" And Mrs. Tigue or Levitski's heads might emerge from kitchen windows to say, "How'd you boys learn to holler so sweet?" or Mrs. O'Keefe who once came out on the front stoop to say, "Weenie Brain is grounded for twenty-five years. You all can run along now."

Though Sonja was a girl and only twelve, she was allowed to accompany the gang of boys because she was an extension of her brother (she idolized him and he respected her for that) but also because she had a new friend whom they thought looked like a movie star. Where was the friend now? She was supposed to be on Ash Road this morning because they were

going to ride bikes down to Black Angel Bridge where a rope
swing was tied to a branch of an old oak by the river. You
could climb the nailed steps on the tree's trunk and reach the
thick rope that burned your hands when you held to it swinging toward the river. You'd fly out and up into the sky, and if
you didn't let go and fall into the water you'd swing back and
slam into the trunk of the tree at top speed and probably die.
The necessity of letting go was a fierce thrill, especially the
first time, when the water below looked very far away and for
a moment the idea of falling into the fast-flowing river was
more frightening in its immediacy than the thought of swinging back toward the trunk. But if you didn't let go, if you
hesitated for even a second, those on land screamed at you at
the top of their lungs, terror in their voices masked by their
irritation at your stupidity. "Let go! Jesus Christ!" The first
time Sonja swung out she didn't let go, couldn't, until the
rope was on its way back to the tree; when she did let go she
was above the shallow part of the river. She dropped down
and felt the thick mud below her feet send a jolting shudder
through her leg bones. She'd walked out of the river amid
jeers and exasperated laughter and "Why didn't ya let go?"
But all of that died a quick death because the next one to
swing out was Carmella—the movie star. Carmella swung
out above the water with a sky-piercing squeal, her body a
smaller version of the bodies in the magazines they were always burying and unearthing in the woods, the ones they
stole from their fathers or bought from Matson Run Drugstore
from a blind man named Kurt, who'd tell them, "Don't think I
don't know what you're looking at."

Carmella managed to smile as she swung out squealing—
they would remember her entering the sky. She wore a simple
blue T-shirt "to bring out my eyes," she told Sonja, and shorts
that Sonja's mother said "might as well be underwear." She
let go on time and fell into the water screaming. When she

emerged from the river she shook water from her ears and held her hair back from her face, then folded her arms while her teeth chattered and they complimented her on letting go. Then she went to sit alone on a rock and smiled, her eyes lowered. Sonja walked over and joined her, the sun through the trees warming their legs. When Carmella rolled her T-shirt up on her stomach, the boys called over, "Take it off!"

"Would you guys stop being ignorant, please?" Carmella yelled, smiling. Sonja lay back and closed her eyes against the sun. The voices calling back and forth from rock to tree were distant arches above her. For a moment she felt homesick for something she couldn't name, and then she knew she only wanted to be smaller, younger, playing cards in a blue room with an old friend, a girl who had moved away a year ago, a girl she had once thought she couldn't live without.

"Ya know the Browntown girl and Reno are going to run away, don't you?" Carmella was saying.

"How do you know?" Sonja said, forgetting everything but Reno and the girl for a moment. She could not hear their names without feeling flushed.

"I don't, but wouldn't you if you were them? Would you stay with a mother who made you scrub the sidewalk on your hands and knees? Not only that, she has to go to six o'clock Mass every day and learn Latin and if she wants to see Reno she's gotta jump out her bedroom window—"

"Hey Carmella!" John called over. "Come on and take a swing again!" Carmella sprung up.

"Well come on," he said. She left the rock and went to climb the steps on the tree.

Sonja stayed on the rock and closed her eyes again. She listened to Carmella's scream, her loud splash, her swimming back to the bank, and then she was on the rock again, shivering and wet. She immediately began to talk about her new school shoes. Sonja looked at the sky and listened, taking refuge in the description, which was so finely detailed, told with such concentrated enthusiasm, and such a contrast to the enormity of sky, that she reached over and touched Carmella's foot with her own. Carmella pulled her foot away and sat up.

They had waited over twenty minutes for her. More than they'd have waited for each other. "Carmella!" they shouted every so often toward the woods. She lived on the other side of them; sometimes she took the path and would suddenly appear at the edge of it as if in a doorway.

"Come on, let's just go," someone said.

"Two more minutes," John said.

And after one minute she came riding leisurely down the gray road on a yellow bike with a flowered banana seat and windblown streamers on the handlebars. She weaved from one side of the road to the other, as if her tires wanted to touch as much road as possible.

"Come on!" Sonja yelled.

Carmella looked too large for the bike, legs too long, torso too tall and full. She reduced it to a yellow toy a lucky younger girl might get on Christmas. Watching her approach filled some of them with an awareness of the world they were losing, an eagerness to get that loss over with once and for all. She finally reached them.

"Hey guys," she said. "This bike sucks, so we can't go too fast, OK?"

Everyone exchanged looks of appreciation. Today she wore denim shorts that she'd decorated herself with a magic marker: peace signs, hearts, smiley faces, flowers, her own name. On her feet were the shoes she'd described to Sonja, the platforms that made her inches taller. Her sweatshirt was the same red as the red in the shoes and the red on her lips. She'd said to Sonja: "In September I always haul out the lipstick."

....

"OK, let's go," John said, headed to Black Angel Dam, riding slowly so Carmella wouldn't be lost. They circled around each other on ten-speeds, some riding with no hands and leaning back, their arms crossed. When they got to the steep, tree-lined hill that led into the valley, they hunched forward and gripped the handlebars and everyone flew squinting into the blue wind at top speed down the hill, and before they had time to wish this part of the ride would never end, it ended. At the bottom of the hill they rode into a lot where an old man sat smoking on a log, talking to himself. They circled before him silently and then left the lot and headed for the second hill that was less steep, but longer. In the distance they could hear dogs howling in the valley. Above them clouds were passing over the sun now; this darkened the thick leaves on the trees and made the road seem like a shadowy tunnel until the sun would shine again and they would feel their own faces, bathed in it.

Sonja watched the back of John's legs, the hard calf muscles pumping as he rose up off the bike to pedal hard the distance of the next road, which had no hills and stretched out like a long, endless hallway. Trees on either side were tall, narrow conifers, ancient and perfectly spaced so that you could look between them and see the flat field beyond like a secret room where goldenrod blazed and made the sky even bluer. The road was miles long.

"Hey, we're takin' a different way. This isn't the road we wanted."

"I've gone this way before. It'll get us there," John said, "And I'll show you this old shack up ahead Reno and me found."

"Wait up!" Carmella yelled. John circled back behind her, and everyone followed, and Sonja wondered if he'd do the same for her, were she to fall behind. She didn't want to find out.

Then she was thinking of Reno, grounded, alone in his room, longing for the girl. She could see his eyes closing on his recent memories, his window looking out on slow-moving trains.

Up ahead on a navy blue bike, riding alone, was Neal. He looked to the side between trees at the goldenrod and rode with no hands. Once, through Woolworth's front window, Sonja had seen him sitting at the lunch counter with his mother in her nurse uniform. He had looked unhappy, withdrawn. The simple memory meshed with the sight of him now on his bike, and she was filled with an awareness of him that felt like hunger.

"Check it out!" a boy named Joey Marina yelled. He rode right in front of Sonja and pointed up ahead to a blonde girl riding a red bike. She had been walking in the field, her bike parked between trees, but it looked to them as if she'd appeared out of thin air.

"Hey," Elroy Caines said. "It looks like that girl we saw in Thriftway last week!"

Everyone was riding faster now. John and Neal were in the lead, looking at the girl, then over at each other, then back at the girl. When Carmella yelled "Wait!" John said, "Somebody give her a ride. Leave your bike here, Carmella, and we'll get it later."

"I'll give you a ride," two of them offered.

The group slowed down and waited while she threw her bike down on the side of the road and hopped on Eddie Tryon's small black seat. Now they were all flying again, and the girl was going just as fast, and Sonja was thinking, *I'd rather be somewhere else. Not here.*

"That's not the Thriftway girl. Her hair wasn't that blonde," John said.

The girl they'd seen in Thriftway (they'd go there to suck the nitrous oxide out of whipped cream canisters—Reno's

....

idea) had written her phone number on a little sheet of paper which John had left in his jeans. The number faded in the laundry.

"Hey, wait up!" they tried yelling, but she was still too far away. They could see her white-blonde hair flying behind her like a flag. The sun made it bright as light itself, the wind whipped it back from her face. They could see her legs, long and brown from the sun. She turned and looked back at them for a second.

"We can ask her to go to the rope swing," Neal said.

Carmella was laughing and shrieking in her attempt to hold onto Eddie, who rode standing up like the others. Sonja watched her grab him around the waist tightly, her face lined against his back, her legs outstretched away from the bike like stiff wings. Each of her shrieks was louder than the last.

They seemed to be gaining no ground. "She must have one of them racing bikes," someone said, breathless. "She's flyin'."

But they were flying too. Their breath was heavy. Sonja watched a swarm of blackbirds breaking in the sky above them and nearly crashed into the boy in front of her. "Wake up," he told her. "Jesus." She kept on pedaling, and now it was like pedaling against her desire to stop, her desire to turn around and ride slowly in the opposite direction.

She looked ahead at the girl and felt certain that they'd never catch her.

"She's too fast," Sonja said.

Nobody agreed or disagreed; nobody wasted their breath.

The gray road was flat and smooth and pouring itself out below them like endless water where the sun glinting off the bicycle spokes danced above the spinning shadows. It was slowly becoming one of those days that even a child suspects memory will claim; in the silence they stole glances at each other as if to ensure memory would be peopled. The tops of the tall trees carved a narrow blue slice of sky above them that might have been another road. Sonja kept seeing it that way, and made herself dizzy.

It finally seemed they might be catching up. They hooted wildly when John said, "Another minute or so. She's tired."

The conscious effort of their pedaling had long since become a pure rhythm, and their bodies were light with it. They fell silent again, aware of the sound of breathing, their own and others'. The girl was slowing down. They saw her hand push her hair back. Her red bike was no racing bike; it was a three-speed at best. How she'd gone so fast they'd never know. Again her hand pushed her hair back, and she turned for a split second and looked back at them. This was the fuel that broke their rhythm; they rose off their seats and knew they'd soon reach her.

"Hey you!" they yelled now. And it seemed as if she was going to turn around for a moment. Instead, she rose up off her seat and pedaled furiously—an invitation, a tease. The wind whipped through her pink T-shirt that hung down longer than her shorts.

Carmella began singing a pop song that had been popular all summer long. Her voice was childish, off-key.

The blonde girl suddenly slammed on her brakes and jumped off her bike and ran into the field of goldenrod, where she stood as if frozen, facing the sky, her back to the road.

They parked their bikes near where she had thrown hers down. On the way into the field, Sonja saw that the girl's spokes were decorated with faded baseball cards, old clothes-pins holding them in place. The back wheel was still spinning slowly.

In the field they circled around her now, and the sight of her was like a long, slow-motion slap in the face, she was so homely. Nobody spoke. Now they looked not at her, but at

each other, their eyes groping, and they began to laugh. Sonja
looked out at the road.

"Hi," the girl said. Her small eyes looked down. She was so
much a betrayal of who they'd been following, they felt she'd
tricked them on purpose. Even the hair was a trick—jagged
dark roots ran down her scalp like a wound. Her long fingers
ended in bright red nails so long they curled at the ends. Now
she appeared to be ordering her own eyes to look at each of
them, one at a time, but they did not see this; they were looking at each other again, getting ready to go. When the girl
found Sonja's eyes they settled there. Sonja felt the others
walking away now, laughing and beginning to talk to each
other. Finally their laughter grew loud, unrestrained, and they
began to bark and howl—their judgment of the girl—as they
made their way down the road.

"Ugly cunt!"

"What a fuckin' dog!"

"Stay off the road, Bleach Job!"

Sonja willed herself to pretend nothing had happened.

"We were wondering if you'd come to a rope swing
with us."

"What the hell you doing back there?" John yelled.
"Come on!"

"I'll be there soon!"

It was not easy to look at the girl. Sonja felt a collision of
emotion inside of her, anger the only one she understood
enough to identify, and so it took precedence. She masked it
and made herself return the girl's odd smile. "Where's the
swing?" the girl said. Her voice was high and clear. She had no
chin. Her thick nose was sunburned and seemed to divide her
face into halves.

"Sonja, come on!" That was Carmella.

"Hold it!" Sonja yelled back. The girl stepped back and

looked down at her feet. She held her hands behind her back and smiled oddly, her small eyes widened.

"Don't," Sonja said. The girl looked up. The gray eyes were trapped, urgent, pleading something.

"You can climb a tree and swing on a rope and fall into the river," Sonja said. She spoke in a monotone, and looked over the girl's shoulder. She wanted her to say "no" and ride away.

"Really? It sounds fun," the girl said. Her ravaged skin was splotched with rouge and thick brown makeup, but it was still possible to see she was blushing. Her eyes were circled with bright blue glittering shadow. On the front of her shirt she'd drawn smiley faces.

"Sonja, we're leavin'!" they yelled.

"Coming!" she yelled back. "So are you coming, or what?" she said to the girl. Now she felt the girl trying to meet her eyes, but she refused. She looked off into the field.

"Good-bye now," the girl said.

"What?"

"Good-bye now."

Their eyes met for a moment before Sonja turned away and walked to get her bike. "I said good-bye now," the girl said again, and when Sonja turned around she saw the same unnerving smile.

When she reached the others there was a hole forming in her stomach. The hole was hot, then cold, then hot again.

They all asked her what she was doing back there talking to the "grit." She shrugged. She pedaled hard, staring ahead.

"Did ya ask her when the last time she washed her face was?"

"That wasn't a face, Neal, that was a pizza," John said.

"She can always just walk backwards for the rest of her life."

Everyone laughed. They rode along. Carmella was singing a song again. They teased her about her voice. "If lovin' you is wrong, I don't wanna be right," she crooned, slightly off-key, and laughed along with them as she sang.

"We weren't very nice," Sonja ventured as they approached Black Angel Dam. If anyone heard, they didn't respond. What could that matter now? Now there was the rope swing, the sun on the river, the slick green leaves still clinging to the trees in the last of the year's warmth, their white undersides turning up in the wind, their splashing and hissing when the wind grew stronger, like it was now. And they parked their bikes on the flat bank near the path that led to the tree fort. Two of the boys headed down the path toward the tree fort to get something, they said, and the rest headed to the swing.

Carmella and John were walking into the woods behind the rope swing now and the others teased them, saying, "I wonder what they're walking into the woods for?"

When someone mentioned Reno, the sound of his name left Sonja cold.

One by one they climbed the tree and swung out and up into sky and let themselves fall into the river. This time Sonja didn't hesitate. She let go of the rope and closed her eyes as she fell and smacked the water. She was underwater now, sinking, and the image of the girl was under there too, her trapped eyes, her presence permeating the floor of the river, the water itself. How long could I hold my breath? Sonja wondered, and began to count in her head and heard the girl's high voice counting along with her, bubbles rising from her lips as she mouthed the numbers. Sonja counted to fifty before kicking her way to the surface, out into the bright air, coughing. Through blurred eyes she saw them all on the bank, bare-chested, staring at her. "We thought you drowned or something!" Neal shouted. With rage, she spat water from her mouth, then swam to shore fast, as if to escape her anger and the girl, propelled by an energy that would leave both in her wake.

"You all right?" Neal asked when she neared shore.

All right?

"Yes, I'm fine," she said, listening to the note in her voice. She rose out of the water, skin glistening in the sun, and smiling, walked toward them.

Replacement

....

➤ Sometimes Doreen couldn't believe that she was still living in a room she would never have seen were it not for the night that she followed him. But he was gone, long gone. Now it was just her and the girl, Katrina. And yesterday, in the light of a morning moon, she had cut her own hair to look like the girl's so that next time they ventured into the street strangers out there might think *mother and daughter*. The hair was piled in the corner now, a dark mound on the green wood floor.

The girl was eleven, playing a toy xylophone in the corner, seated on the edge of the cot. She wore a man's sleeveless undershirt like a dress and on the back of it with a black pen (she called it an ink pen and would let nobody touch it) she'd drawn a huge sun and the words KILL ROACHES in the middle of it in back-slanting letters she said was proof of talent. "I could go into lettering one day," she'd said, out of the blue.

"Katrina," Doreen said.

"Name's Frank."

"Frank, your mother's not coming back and neither is Isaiah-Ahmed." (*Beautiful man,* she added in her mind. Even his abandoning her could not bring the rage that might have punctured love.)

"We could go lookin' for them again," said the girl. "One more time."

"They're not in the city anymore. I can feel it in my bones."

The girl pushed the toy instrument off of her lap; the bright metal keys crashed to the floor, a few high notes clinking. "I'm sick-a-ya feelin' it in your bones!" she said.

"Katrina, don't holler. I'm nervous enough."

The girl walked to the high window where the moon could be seen resting on the dark apartment building across from them, scattered rectangular windows brimming with orange light. She had to tiptoe to see out. Doreen applied another coat of lipstick, thinking *When, Lord, when* will the emptiness go away? She looked up at the flaking ceiling and watched two roaches circle the light, side by side, so parallel it was almost for a split second pretty.

"No whales in the sky now," the girl said. "They all got smart and swam off to a better place."

"No doubt."

Earlier they had watched the schools of dark clouds swimming across the moon as if swallowing it. The bright ball of light had burst through the gray whales to get back to the sky, leaving behind groping tatters with illuminated edges. Katrina had played her xylophone, her eyes held wide on that sky. At one point she smiled, the tension of her face vanishing. Doreen had wanted to take a picture of that, it was so rare.

The night Doreen had first walked off the street, down the alley and up the fire escape into the battered room that was turning out to be some kind of temporary home, was the night she had tired of cows. She had gone to visit them for so long after James died, a weekly ritual, taking the bus out of the city (avoiding the cemetery though it was what had given her a taste for country air), her own reflection floating in the tinted bus window above the road. There had been a child that night who kept asking Why? no matter what the fancy mother said, the mother refusing to acknowledge the child's attempt to irritate or amuse, responding to each Why? as if it were sincere and answerable. (Doreen could still hear the woman saying "Because Daddy thinks trout fishing's the next best thing to dying and going to heaven, that's why, damn it.") And with that the child had lost control: Why! Why! Why! she'd shouted, and would not stop, until every rider on the bus felt the shame and sadness of the child breaking down, all rage and tears, and Doreen thinking, I would like to have that child, I would.

It was always a good thing, stepping off the bus into the utterly foreign smell of grass and manure, starred breath of earth gathering around her like a cape from a different world, the bus pulling away and herself in the white dress splashed with violets that James had bought in another city before his sickness was even named. She would turn to watch the spewed clouds of exhaust, vanishing.

She had bent down and picked up a white stone that night and held it tightly, walking up the road. When the face of James rose in her it usually took her along like a chill, but that night his image was strangely powerless, and she felt the memory as habit, the sadness more like weariness. It terrified her. She whispered his name. James? James? She tried to wind her grief back in as one tries to pull down a kite. But it was as if she'd lost the ball of string, and the kite had flown behind the stars, and her hands ached, they were so newly empty. They were like someone else's hands, suddenly attached to her wrists. She held them up and looked at them, her heart drumming loudly inside her head. And then her entire body responded to a moment's dream of ascension. A moment's dream.

She walked on toward the farm where the cows were kept, her eyes on Edgel's house, the white door standing in the stone, long and moonlit. An old fear overwhelmed her—the house was suddenly a house tucked away in her memory; she saw herself as a child being sent to live with odd relatives, a suitcase packed with her favorite things—red Thermos full of stones, rag doll, a blue dress that later in a dream Katrina would wear before turning into a bird, and two Almond Joys she'd planned on sharing, already melted.

"So you're Doreen," the taller aunt had said, stepping back with critical eyes to appraise, as if to find an essence inside of her that would invite a grown man's touch. And in the house an unhappy smell and wax fruit on the table. "Tell us about yourself," the younger aunt said. The two women were on the couch, facing her on the small red chair as if she were an awaited means of transportation that had arrived on time, but damaged.

"I'm nine," she had told them. What else was there to say? *Not to drown.* To be a grown woman walking toward my cows. She was then beginning to sense that this would be the last night of visiting. She saw Edgel, the farmer, a thin man walking toward his white shed with rope in his arms. "Edgel!" she cried, but he was too far off. The loss of James began to seem pristine and absolute, and her stomach was cold.

Was there an animal, small and shivering at the edge of the woods with a human face? (And why did no thought startle?)

She had moved then beyond all astonishment, save the sudden consciousness of loneliness, how fierce it had grown, how it had made her strange in her own eyes, and worse, someone whom James might hardly recognize. Was part of grief's cruelty to change the bereaved into someone the dead would think strange? For days in the mirror her eyes had looked too luminous. Once, she had seen the echo in her brain reflected around her head like a dark halo.

She walked up to the sagging fence and faced the cows that night. Good-bye to twenty-one black Angus. They were soaked in moonlight so brilliant it seemed violent. She stared at them, silenced, and they stared back, their souls in their eyes (or so she had once thought), apprehending the future, yearning to escape into some sleeker form and head down the road at top speed screaming. She had perhaps come to see the cows so regularly because they taught her something of the body's limitations. In a gifted moment she had understood why they were holy and sacred elsewhere. How impossible it was to really look at a cow and not imagine something caught inside that flesh. The body was a prison, and a cow could teach you that the way a graceful deer never could.

And yet the body is the body is the self, is what she might have said that last night, had she words for her body's knowledge. She remembered the week before, the white birds scattered around the cows like the cow's ideas; inside the ideas lived the warning that she didn't belong *there* either. For all their peace, they were impenetrable, might even be mocking her ritual visits. "I won't come again, good-bye," she had told them finally, then walked to Edgel's front door. The ground felt too soft below her feet.

Edgel had been a contact of sorts; she had gone once with him to a bar in the sticks called Kings and Queens, barstools with backs like greasy fur-covered thrones, and neither of them had been able to think of much to say, so they'd stirred their drinks and lifted their faces to the TV, where an apparently exciting football game was being played; the others in the bar had their hearts in it. In the end, their mutual lack of love for the sport had bonded them, hadn't it? Hadn't their silence grown comfortably deep in opposition to the crowd's exuberance? She would remember how he told her in the truck, "You're a real nice lady, but we're not from the same world. You'll meet a nice fella someday soon, and I'll meet a nice lady, a bit older named Lucinda or Louise, an *L* name." And she hadn't said, "Why an *L* name?" nor did he explain the significance. So she rode, pretending to understand, so desperately whole-hearted that it almost felt like real understanding. It became, for a short while, her attitude toward the world.

She knocked that last night on his door, trying to peer through limp curtains into the kitchen. He swung it open and stood with a bottle of half-emptied Scotch in his hand, a tall woman in her sixties standing beside him in shoes most often seen on police. The woman had long hair that she pushed behind her ears.

"I came to say good-bye," Doreen said, and felt the surprising loss of his singleness drop through her like a rock into a pit.

"Enter, honey, and meet Marguerite," he said. The three of them had a glass of Scotch in a low-ceilinged kitchen that smelled like a garage. Pictures of another decade's starlets were taped onto the walls, their old edges curling up as if protecting themselves. "She loves the cows," Edgel explained to Marguerite. "I told her not to go gettin' attached to any one of 'em in particular," he laughed. Marguerite raised a curious eyebrow.

"I'm staying in the city from now on," Doreen explained, and Edgel said he could understand why; she was a fish out of water in these parts.

Did he care?

Marguerite poured more Scotch, crossed her long legs, and sighed. Doreen saw the two wink at each other, and the single gesture made the echo in her brain so loud that when it came time to say good-bye she heard her own voice as one who wakes in the night to the siren of an ambulance, thinking *Whoever it is, help them, God.*

"I'm starved," Doreen told the girl, finishing pretzels, and recalled her mother's "Don't say 'starved,' you don't even know *hungry* much less starved," and her pulling out the worn manila envelope packed full of tragedies, including the bodies of dying black children photographed in magazines, ribs under skin like steps the eyes climbed to get to the faces. "Look at these children," her mother had said. "You think they don't dream?" And Doreen had merely nodded when her mother went to the state hospital, only to be visited, never to come home, a woman pumped full of Thorazine on the sixth floor, stupidity replacing terror. "So how the hell is school?" she'd say, laughing in the stale light, winking as if there were secrets being shared.

Doreen had even told Ahmed *that*. Even James had not caused so much memory to rise so quickly.

"What I mean is, I'm hungry," she told the girl, who was curled on the cot now, having exhausted herself in front of the washstand mirror trying to make a cowlick in her hair.

"And not for another damn donut," she added.

"I could live off air and water," the girl mumbled. "If I had to, I could live alone in the park and eat leaves and fruit. I don't need a bed, or donuts, or french fries, or shoes, even." She was always listing the things she could do without. It was almost a prayer.

"You're a growing girl. You need milk and the like, and certainly shoes. Streets like these would kill your feet."

"I'm a growing boy," said the girl, and yawned. "I'm a wild-cat boy."

"It's not good to pretend too much," Doreen told her. "You'll forget you're pretending. That's how people get outlandish." Then she added her father's words when she'd been small: "All the lights are on, but there's nobody home." But the image of his face folded in on itself, stopping thought.

"Soon we gotta go to work," Doreen reminded the girl.

"I know."

"You've been a big help to me," Doreen said.

"I know."

The room was filling up with gray light. Doreen lit a cigarette. "My mother wanted a gun," said the girl. "In the middle of the night she'd get up on a chair and scream her lungs out if there was a rat. And once she smacked one with her clarinet."

136

"That's too bad," Doreen said, growing uncomfortable. "Play something on the xylophone. Something to start the day," she told the girl, who didn't move, her green eyes staring into space, then closing.

Doreen got into her work uniform. The white polyester pants itched and the pink blouse would never stop smelling of do-nuts no matter how long it soaked. And she had to wear a cap, also pink; it was too large for her head, and the peak of it nearly covered her eyes if she wasn't consistent about adjusting it. Sometimes she would tilt her head back just to see. Every-one at the donut shop had to wear this outfit except the girl, whose only job was to clean out the glaze bins and ride on the delivery truck with Doreen, making sure the racked donuts in the back didn't slide off the metal shelves.

Katrina dressed in brown corduroys, held up too high on her waist by a thin black belt pulled to the final notch. She kept the undershirt on, though it was tucked in and hidden by the snow coat she wore, a green quilted nylon jacket with ribbed cotton cuffs and a detachable hood that zipped up the middle. She detached the hood, then wore it anyway.

Doreen locked the door of the room after making it almost tidy, arranging lipstick tubes on the blue dresser near the metal candelabrum Ahmed had left behind, Katrina setting the xylo-phone under her cot near her rocks. Doreen had stripped the beds and hung the sheets on the thin rope she'd stretched across the room near the ceiling. Air that was not fresh, but better than nothing, came into the room each day and took their old dreams out of the sheets (the girl's belief) so they could have fresh dreams each night. It was why the girl refused to sleep with a pillow; dreams could get caught in the feathers. Still, sometimes she cried out in her sleep, and once when her arms flailed the air Doreen had to wake her and tell her where she was. Katrina's stunned eyes stayed open for hours after that; she sat on the cot, rocking back and forth with a terrible energy. Doreen sat beside her, afraid that the child might go on rocking forever.

"I bet we see a clue today," Katrina said, from the back of the donut truck, an old step-van with newly painted sky blue walls. It was raining. Doreen pretended she hadn't heard the girl and concentrated on avoiding collisions; the streets in the dark morning were already chaotic, cars and people darting like there were no rules. In the rearview she saw Katrina stuff a cream donut into her mouth, her black hair still slicked down and side-parted like a boy's under the green hood. "Taste good?" she said, meaning, really, I love you.

She remembered the first time she'd seen the girl (it was not even months and seemed years ago) there in Ahmed's room.

After the cows and Edgel, she had taken the bus back to the city, thinking she would spend some money, cheer herself up a bit, fill time so she wouldn't have to go home alone to the room where she'd lived with James. She walked the streets, stopping here and there to look at magazines, cosmetics, candy, and all of it looked like goods from another world. She drank a cup of black coffee at a dim cafe where an old man directly outside her window played the saxophone, his instrument pointed to the sky, his eyes closed. She closed her own eyes, and for a while there was nothing in the world but coffee and music. Finally a white-faced waiter had nudged her, saying, "Earth calling. You'll have to leave, ma'am, or order something to eat."

She left. She crossed the street, her arms folded, her eyes peering ahead at a corner market, her tongue touching the roof of her mouth which the hot coffee had burned. The night air was cool on her skin; she shivered against it.

The outside of the market was lined with piles of beautifully arranged fruit, lit by streetlight except for the melons, dark in the awning shade. Under one of the highest wooden tables where newly sprayed grapes gleamed, a woman wrapped in a filthy blanket sat swaying, her thumb in her mouth, headlights streaking her. Doreen looked away to the left and into the eyes of the man who stood beside her, an arm's length away, a maroon apple in his dark hand.

Though their eyes had met for just a moment, the contact seemed prolonged somehow. She looked down at the apple, struck by the hand, the beautiful strength of the fingers. She moved toward the next table, feeling the man was watching her, though when she stole a glance she found he was not. He was placing the apple into a brown paper bag and moving toward the pears, his square back to her in a black shirt. *From someplace I've never heard of,* she had thought the instant their eyes had met. What had affected her was their expression, and though she had no words to describe the moment, something in her was already trying to relive it. Again he turned around and looked at her, with no expectation, and no defense, the black eyes in the face that for another prolonged moment made the rest of the world a periphery, receding.

She looked away and he walked into the store. She stood near the pears, picked one up, and pretended to examine its bruises with her fingers. The next pear she dangled by its stem, holding it near her face as she watched him through the lit doorway, the way he waited in line, his eyes downcast, squinting a bit. She watched him speak to the clerk and then knew with certainty (though she could never have explained the source of the knowledge) that he was a man who lived alone (his room seemed to gather around him, the order of it something he worked hard to maintain, a tropical plant on the radiator dying). He had lived alone for a long time; that was clear. She drank in the precision of his gestures—nothing wasted, as if a great energy were being willed into place, controlled, saved, yes, and incredible silence was trailing him.

Most of all, there was his face.

It was the effort in his face that captivated her, perhaps even more than his eyes had looking into hers. The effort reflecting what seemed an enormous struggle to be present, to peer through the brain's echo and thank the clerk sincerely in this world. She saw the profile of his quick smile (he almost winced when he looked at people, as though he saw light). And now he was walking toward the lit door, squinting slightly, blinking twice in a sort of nervousness. He passed by her—one more look in the eye which may as well have been an embrace. And following him on the sidewalk she knew thick blue veins branched in his brown arms where he held the bag of fruit. He did not look back to encourage her, and yet she could feel the inevitability of what was happening, desire so deep it dispelled all fear; she imagined he was somehow pulling her along.

They kept an even pace, him nearly a half block ahead of her, people streaming through him, then the same people streaming through her. She imitated the way he held his head perfectly straight, imagining he saw only the night air the way she saw only his back in the black shirt.

She walked this way, block after block. When he paused to cross the jammed narrow streets, she too stopped, right in the middle of the sidewalk; anyone watching would've imagined her in the grips of realizing she'd forgotten something, would have expected her to head back in the direction from which she'd come. But he would cross over, and she would walk again, her eyes holding on.

He was stopping now, or slowing down, turning off the street at last into an alley, and now her pace quickened. She reached the mouth of the alley; he was not in sight, but she heard footsteps on iron and saw the alley lead to a moonlit courtyard, and on the ground against the wall to her left an old flowered shoe lay in the litter near a beer can. She looked

....

down at the miniature faded roses until the sound of footsteps ceased.

"I see him, I see him, go left! It's Ahmed!" the girl screamed. The rain was turning to snow, and Doreen took the left too quickly; dozens of donuts flew off the racks. She pulled the truck over to the curb, her heart slamming. "Where?"

The girl, looking out the back window, said it was just some guy who looked like him. "Whoops," she added.

Doreen looked in the rearview at the donuts all over the filthy metal floor—the grime and butts and dust and donuts. "Clean up there, damn it, or my ass is *fired!*" she yelled.

"I'm sorry," Katrina said. "I was seein' things."

"Yeah, seein' things. Where's this thing you were seein'?" The girl pointed ahead to a coatless stranger in a yellow hat who smoked a cigar out on the sidewalk. He was half the size of Ahmed.

"Seein' things," Doreen said. "Jesus."

"I'm sorry," Katrina said. "I *said* I'm sorry."

Doreen turned around and looked at her. The serious white face in the green hood looked defeated, even younger than usual, and suddenly exhausted.

Back in the room that night, Doreen read a cookbook she'd bought on sale, full of foods she'd never heard of, while Katrina stood in front of the mirror, saying, "If I walked down the street now, nobody from my other life would know who I was except my mother." She wore a Cleveland Brown's cap bought for a quarter in a thrift store.

"Katrina?" Doreen said.

"Who's that?" said the girl.

"Frank," Doreen said. "You OK tonight?"

"Yes."

"The hat looks good. You look like a real good boy."

The girl sighed and took the cap off. "I bet you Ahmed's married to another woman," she said. "A real pretty one. And he forgot you was alive, he don't even think of you, you won't see him again, ever."

Doreen looked down at Katrina's feet, toes curling on the wood. "Maybe you're right," she said. Her face felt hot.

"This ain't our home. We ain't home."

"So leave," Doreen said. She closed the cookbook and looked at Katrina. The girl stared back at her, wide-eyed.

"If you wanna leave, by all means leave."

The girl looked up at the ceiling. "No. But tomorrow I'm goin' out to look again. Not ridin' in the stupid shit donut truck."

"Good, fine," Doreen said. "I don't blame you a bit."

There were times when Doreen tried to recount, moment by moment, how she had entered the room. The child's red bike on its side in the courtyard. The gray dog watching from the corner, its eyes almost yellow. The light flicking on and the man above her there in the window, setting the bag of fruit on the sill. He was looking down, but had he seen her?

She saw him start to take off his shirt, just a slice of bare chest, and then she was on the iron steps, ascending. Halfway up she felt the window light beside her and turned, and though he looked at her with the same expression he had at the market, now she was terrified. But he had opened the window, the generosity in his face seeming to increase. "Hello," he said. "Are you visiting me? Use the door," he pointed.

And hours later, seeing his body whole in the dark, a glass of water in his hand like light, she would feel the gratitude (so thorough it transformed) known only to those who have sensed themselves as undeserving in the presence of beauty.

And he seemed unaware of the contrast they made while she saw him more clearly than she would have had she mirrored this beauty.

This was after talking. After she told him about Edgel, losing Edgel, as if the farmer had been her lover. The name of James, the fact of death, she had not uttered until later, when the words spilled out of her so easily she felt she had found someone she'd been born to talk to.

And he had listened, as if with every cell in his body, as if to teach her the meaning of listening. Real listening was something you could *hear*.

What came to her most often was the memory of him above her, looking down, layers and layers, opening. "What can I do for you?" he'd said.

"Just stay here like this," she'd tried to say, but the one word emerging was *this*.

He had brought her back to the beginning of herself; every touch felt like a reshaping.

She would try to stand up, weak-kneed, fingers moving to touch the tiny dots of color in the dark, Ahmed handing her the glass of water.

On the second night, late, he had given her a robe to wear; old and flannel with a gray print of coyotes in the mountains. They sat talking and drinking Night Train wine from glasses flecked with old paint; Doreen thought them pretty—a snowstorm.

"My father was a drover," he said, and before she could ask what a drover was, a knock came to the door.

"Ah-med? Ah-Meddy?" The voice was a bark. "You in there?"

And before he could answer, the voice added, "Mother of God, tell what's happening."

"My neighbor across the hall," Ahmed told Doreen, getting up and walking to the door, sheet wrapped around his waist. He opened it to the dim light of the hall, and Doreen saw a hand reach up and settle on his shoulder. "Heart," the voice said. "Give a lady what she needs. Just one."

"I ran out."

"No more?"

"I got only aspirins."

"Well, invite us the hell in," the woman said.

Doreen sat further back on the bed, leaning against the wall in the dark, her body braced.

"I have a friend," Ahmed said, and the woman said, "Don't we all."

The next second, she and Katrina were in the room, the girl's hair that night resembling the black-penned rays she'd later drawn around the sun on her undershirt. Ahmed bent over and kissed her head, and the woman, seeing Doreen, said, "He's the only man my baby lets come near. He's special." Doreen nodded. Ahmed lit the three candles on the dresser. The woman lit a cigarette. Then Ahmed took Katrina's hand and walked her over to the front corner of the room. He put his hands on either side of her head, tilted it upward, and said something to her very quietly. He said something else, and she laughed. In the dim moon and silence they were people underwater.

Then they were looking out the window, the girl tiptoed beside him. "It's called a 'gibbous' moon when it's like that," Doreen heard him say. "Meaning more than half and not quite whole." The girl said, "Gibbous." And then they turned from the window and faced Doreen while the woman began pacing as if she were ready to make a speech, one hand on her chin and the other waving the lit cigarette in frantic circles.

Finally Ahmed introduced the girl as Katrina, and the woman pointed to herself and said, "And I'm her mother, Grace Demain," then sat down on the floor, refusing the folding chair Ahmed offered. She brought her legs up to cover her chest; her arms, bangled, wrapped around her shins, and she rested her chin on her knees. The girl was back in the far corner with her arms crossed. "So why's it so damn quiet?" she wanted to know.

"I don't know," Doreen said, to be friendly.

Ahmed came back to sit beside her now. The woman started laughing loudly, though it sounded more like a cry. She stopped as suddenly as she'd started. "You might not know this," she said, looking at Doreen. "But I'm drunk. I'm so drunk you look like an angel of God. But if I had one of God's blessed pain pills I could pass out good."

"Take four aspirins," Ahmed offered. "It's all I got left."

"Candy shit," the woman barked. And then she introduced herself all over again. "I'm Grace Demain!"—pointing violently at her breastbone. "And that's my little girl Katrina and her father's so fucked up we won't go back again, right honey? I'm a home, you're a home, everyone's a home. We live inside each other, right little girl?"

The girl did not answer. She crouched down on her haunches and pretended to study the green wooden floor.

"When she's shy that means she likes you," her mother said.

Ahmed got up and went to the white washstand on the other side of the room. Doreen could see him reflected in the mirror there. He filled one of the paint-flecked glasses with water and brought it to the woman with some aspirin.

"God bless," she said, and took all the aspirin at once, most of the water dribbling down her face.

Doreen had thought that night: If Grace should ever die, we would take the girl away, comb down her hair, bring her to an indoor pool for swimming lessons. Ahmed could teach us the names of the stars in a quiet place. Then a baby sister would come and I never . . . I would hold . . . I would lean on his arm that way with camels out the window, real fruit on the sills, Katrina healing.

"For Christ's sake, turn the light on," Grace had finally belted out, and Isaiah said no, it hurt the eyes. "Candle man," Grace said, smiling for a moment before one side of her mouth collapsed into a frown while the other side remained up, quivering as if yanked by a fishhook. The girl looked at Doreen and said, "She ain't always like this."

"I know," Doreen said. "Don't worry." And how well she knew the child's need to protect the broken parent from eyes that knew no history and so were cold! An old sense of shame overwhelmed her, and she pulled the sash of the robe tighter.

"She can play the clarinet," the girl said to Doreen.

"And some day, honey, I'll play for you," the woman said, "like Benny Goodman," then curled up into a ball on the floor and sighed, her cheek against the wood. She closed her eyes. The three of them were quiet for a moment, staring down at her as if waiting.

"We could all of us live on bread and water if we had to," Katrina said then and walked over and sat down next to Doreen.

"What kind of damn animal is that?" she asked, pointing to coyotes, two of them lounging on a flat cliff near Doreen's rib. Ahmed helped Grace to her feet. "Let's go home," he said, and moved her toward the door and then across the hall. Katrina sighed, then stood up and walked to the doorway.

"You like Ahmed?" she said, turning around to face Doreen.

"Yes."

"Then I like you."

Now Katrina sat cross-legged on the cot, her back against the wall. She had barely spoken all evening, defeated after having spent another day searching the streets. So many hours of insistent peering had left her eyes looking too large and hungry. Doreen knew too well what the girl's day had been like, strangers in the distance turning into the loved one in fleeting moments of violent expectancy, then the heart sinking again, each sink deeper than the last. This is how the insides of a person were made.

"Why don't you play some music, honey," Doreen said, washing the pink uniform in the sink, avoiding her own face in the mirror.

"Pointless," said the girl.

"You hungry? We could get out of here and get something good to eat."

"Whatever will be fine," Katrina said.

"Will it?"

A silence fell; Doreen stood wringing out the shirt, and Katrina ran her skinny fingers through her hair. "Do you like your father?" she said suddenly. Their eyes met in the mirror for a moment, then Doreen looked down.

"I don't exactly know where he is," Doreen said.

"Is he good?" Katrina said.

"Is he good? Let's see. Well, I just don't know," Doreen said, and turned around, trying to smile. Katrina looked up at the window.

"You don't exactly need a father to have a good life," Doreen said, meaning to be helpful. She blushed at her own remark. It hung in the room, absurd, irrelevant.

"I'm hungry," the girl snapped.

And Doreen remembered how Katrina looked on Ahmed's shoulders two days after her mother disappeared, four days before he left himself. In the park there had been a moment of clarity that etched itself into her mind, his black eyes turned up to see the girl's face bowed down to his, both of them just about to laugh, red light of sky soaring above the ground, then lowering down on them later, as if it could care.

Doreen stared out the window at the apartment building across from them; up high in a lit window a red dress was hanging. In a higher window a woman held a child. Had Ahmed been there, it would've been time to eat now.

He had taken bags of fruit each night and sectioned bright pieces into four portions on blue plastic plates. They had eaten in the room at the end of the hall, a sea green room as narrow as the hallway itself, a door-shaped window looking over the street. And he would say the blessing with his eyes closed, the candelabrum brought from his room on the middle of the table now, lit up.

Then he would give everyone a speckled vitamin tablet. The fruit, wet and sliced in the candlelight, seemed for a moment untouchable.

"Let's all never leave," Katrina said one night, like a second blessing. But Ahmed had put his finger to his lips and said "Shhh," and then, for a moment, Doreen saw that his face held the same expression it wore the night she woke to find him watching her sleep.

And when it came time for him to say good-bye he assured her they would see each other again, and if he could he would explain the reason for his leaving. Understand I love you.

She had held onto him, unable to stop talking. He had not tried to quiet or rush her, had not tried to loosen her hands. And when finally she fell silent, he looked down and asked her please to let him go, as if he could not turn and head toward the long mouth of the alley without her finally resigning, body stiffening as she wished him what? Good luck? Sweet dreams?

If he could stand there forever, a man in a courtyard surrounded by buildings where the windows fall like fire-lit rain . . . how much the sight of his body meant to her—would it always be impossible to say?

Watching him walk away was not difficult. What you don't believe cannot hurt. You must walk back up the fire escape, into the room, fill a glass of water, and drink.

When the knock sounded urgent in the dawn light as she woke from a dream of being lost on a train, Doreen sat up and said, "Who?"

....

But she knew who.

And Grace Demain, holding a plaid suitcase and a clarinet in a plastic see-through bag, was a sober woman with new red highlights in her hair, asking *Where in the world is Ah-med*, then exploding into a flurry of thanks and apology while Katrina, crying with joy, slipped into the brand new coat.

It was deep red with a black velvet collar.

"It's dressy," Katrina said. It came down past her knees and the sleeves were inches too long. "You'll grow into it, Babe," her mother said, and in Doreen's mind it was a man's voice saying, "Pretty little thing, ain't she?"

"Now comb your hair and thank Doreen for everything," her mother said, and Doreen joked that donuts would fly all over hell's creation until she found a good replacement. And then Katrina's things were placed in the plaid suitcase, xylophone on top, and it was all zipped up, and they were walking down the fire escape, Katrina holding tightly to the rusty railing, her wet green eyes peering straight ahead, not looking over at Doreen, who was framed in the window watching the descent.

There were no thoughts in her mind as she swept the green floor and arranged the glasses and Katrina's rocks on the dresser. She put the room in order and gathered her things. The sun was caught in the washstand mirror now, blasting, and the pulse of that sunken light was the last face she saw before closing the door behind her and walking away.

Down in the street, headed back to a room on the other side of the city, she felt like a woman on her way to pay a visit to a dying friend. What was there to say? How had she been? Was she still there at all? There would be photographs curled up in drawers, James's clothes still hanging, their smell, his smell, the feel of his arms still in the sleeves of his shirts. There would be surfaces silvered with months of dust, awaiting her finger, as if there were a word that might be written there before she cleaned. The sidewalk moved below her like a conveyor belt now, and she was filling up with something heavier than tears, and suddenly it stopped her, whatever it was. She let the crowd pour through her, their legs taking them so quickly in so many different directions. The noise of the city may have been deafening, but Doreen heard nothing and stood now, paralyzed. *The things I didn't tell Katrina.* Katrina, you grow out of it, you make room, you give yourself away in pieces or whole, and the man who hurts you early on, love will almost kill him, if you're lucky.

An Evocation

....

➤ The people who have mattered to me have revealed themselves in autumn. This is no coincidence, but rather reflects the fact that in autumn I feel at my strongest, more at home in the world, almost (though never entirely) willing to accept yearning itself as a partner. Which is of course when people come to you. You needn't stay alive too long to learn that just when you've decided you don't need anyone, well, there they are. It's as if you're in a forest when suddenly the wind has died, and the sun raining through open spaces that fallen leaves have left behind is like a spotlight on the ground, and the person who will matter simply steps out from behind a large tree trunk and stands in the patch of brilliant light on the leaves. They look at you. You look at them. It takes only a few of the shyest glances to sense the inevitability of your lives intersecting, meshing. There's really no choice, no chance of a real good-bye after that.

I received the news five months ago. My mother clipped it out of the local paper and sent it two thousand miles through the mail.

On my front stoop, in the thick morning fog, I opened the envelope and read the simple obituary, listing "a short illness" as the cause of her death, noting her career and her survivors,

151

which included her parents and three children, two of whom I'd never seen. Jared, Deirdre, Vincent. I read these names four or five times, my mind working to conjure images of what they looked like. But I could see only their mother's eyes, bright and brown as they looked in childhood, superimposed on vague, childish faces whose other features disintegrated, as if I had no right to even imagine them.

When I looked up through the fog, I saw my daughter on her bicycle, stopped on the sidewalk before me, her face flushed and anxious, her red sweater especially vibrant. "What's the matter?" she asked me—I'd been staring at her as if she were a stranger, I suppose. She did, in these moments, seem a kind of stranger, the way anyone in the present will when the past that didn't include them is suddenly too pressingly vivid. She rang the small silver bell attached to the handlebars, then rang it again, as if to tell me, Come back, recognize me, I'm yours.

"I'm hungry," she said.

"Come get a snack," I told her. "Park your bike in the alley." And an image of my friend as a child on her red bike flying down a narrow, tree-lined road raced through my mind. I was on a bike on another road; we would meet each other halfway by a pond, swim in our underwear, feed ducks.

I gave Brenda her snack, then sat down by my kitchen window and called my mother. I told her I thought it was odd, rude really, to send an obituary in an envelope unaccompanied by a note of some sort. And why hadn't she called me? I'd have surely attended the funeral. My voice broke as I said this. And she said she was frankly surprised at how upset I seemed when, after all, I'd fallen out of touch with Patrice ages ago, hadn't I?

My mother quickly added, "It is terrible she died so young. I remember when the two of you were joined at the hip."

"Do you?"

"So young," she repeated, sighing, and I said I wasn't accustomed to thinking of forty-two as "so young." She laughed. "Take it from me," she said. "You're a babe." She laughed again.

When I hung up, Brenda was looking at me with the expression I hate most to see—a kind of protective, anxious concern in her seven-year-old face, something I never wanted her to feel toward me. But she takes it upon herself to feel this way a lot.

"Who died?" she said, and swallowed hard, her eyes wide and ready to fill up.

"Nobody you knew," I said, and saying that, my heart twisted into a knot; I had always assumed that someday the two of them would meet.

"But who was it?"

"An old friend of mine. Someone I knew when I was little," I told her. "That's all, nothing for you to worry about."

I took the two photographs I have of Patrice and taped them to the wall by my mirror. If there was a bright moon, they would seem charged with life, three-dimensional. On moonless nights, headlights of passing cars would streak over them; she would leap out of the darkness, then recede again when the car was gone.

In one photograph she stands in a pale red dress and sneakers against the white wall of an animal shelter where she worked as a volunteer when she was ten. She squints, smiling into the sunlight, her dark hair pulled back, one ankle crossed over the other.

The other picture is black and white and taken by her father on a summer night the year she was eight. It captures the moment she suddenly stopped running, stopped laughing. Her hair and nightgown fly backwards, she is out of breath, her

....

eyes shine as if astonished. You can look at this picture and can almost hear her breathing with the crickets.

My dreams were full of her. They wouldn't go away.

After a month I decided I'd drive seven hundred miles to the house she grew up in, the house where as a child I spent as much time as I did in my own home and where her parents are still living. I thought I'd visit and offer condolences, and that this could serve as a kind of good-bye. But the closer I got to that house, the more I knew the idea was doomed to remain fantasy. I was afraid of facing them. It had been too long. Who was I to them? I parked over a block away under a towering elm, bright yellow in the black sky, and walked down the narrow street toward her house, past other houses I still knew well, not only their physical structures, but the aura each house had grown when long ago she told me something of the lives the houses sheltered.

"That's where Mr. Vincent lives. He's a loner. He needs some tender mercy. His son committed suicide last year."

And Mr. Vincent's house, as she spoke, was encircled by a barely perceptible darkness, a darkness that was like the smell of metal, his blue door narrowing. I visited him with her when she took to giving him presents—odd things like a pair of her father's socks, or detergent, or a hundred dandelions strung together that later we saw him wearing around his neck, bare-chested in the grocery store.

"And that's where the Chevon's live. Mrs. Chevon's from Latvia and Mr. Chevon knows how to play music on glasses of water, but they have a deaf baby."

Her house sat at the very bottom of the winding hill near the woods, a beautiful stone house with blue shutters and a white door. The sight of it made my heart pound, even as the house looked much smaller and less magical than it did to me as a child. I felt suddenly too large, as if I wouldn't fit through the front door even if I tried.

There were no lights on in the house. I took off my overcoat and pressed my back against the side stone wall and closed my eyes. I stood there inhaling the depths of that particular smell of her yard in late November, the deep leaves layering the ground, the sudden smell of blood we had exchanged in a ceremony of becoming "sisters," poking each of our fingertips with a penknife, then pressing them together, eyes closed.

I walked to the back and stood at the yard's edge near the woods and looked at the sleeping house. It was quite the same. I saw the white ground-level door that led to the tiny room sunk in the earth, an adjunct to the basement where tools or junk might have been stored had she not claimed it as our fort. The floor was dirt, the ceiling low, the stone walls damp and cold. We lit candles in there and set them on the plywood table her father built in the narrow alcove. There were four wooden blue chairs lined at that table where Harriet Tubman and Dred Scott (we made dummies as a history project and grew attached to them) sat between us, taller than us, wearing her parents' old shoes and brown gloves. Our four shadows were sharp on the wall, facing us.

When we had money, we belted Scott and Tubman to our backs and rode them on our bikes down to Woolworth's, where we all four sat at the counter for a snack. I don't think Patrice ever noticed the bemused, indulgent smiles we received when we entered or the irritated looks some of the customers exchanged when Nadine the waitress pretended to take Scott and Tubman's order. But I had an awareness I worked hard to disguise, trying to live up to other people's expectations of my innocence.

And this was the fifties: there were people saying, "Niggers ain't welcome at this counter, even if they are dummies." Patrice would stare at these people, curious; her father had taught her that prejudiced people were "terrified" and "sad."

As I walked toward the door of the sunken room that night, a light flicked on upstairs, insistent as a face. I ran into the woods then, and waited until the house was dark again. It was there in the woods that the strangeness of my own behavior frightened and saddened me. Who would understand this?

I went back to the car, drove for hours, had breakfast at three in the morning in a diner whose windows looked out on a river and knew that the visit had relieved me of nothing. I got home in time to give Brenda pancakes before school and braid her hair. Her face in the round mirror was serious and studied mine. When our eyes met we both smiled quickly, then looked away.

When I was seven, my father dropped my mother and I off at a small urban port at twilight and kissed us quietly good-bye. They had conspired to make it casual for my sake so that I wouldn't suspect the finality of it. But of course children sense these things. Walking away, holding my mother's hand, I kept turning around to look at my father for what was to be the last time. He didn't wave and neither did I. A wave is too frivolous for a final good-bye, I suppose. Behind him on a white ship men on deck looked toy-sized against the sky. My father could've turned, picked them up, and put them in the pockets of his blue jacket.

We bought roasted peanuts from a man in a wooden stand out on the street. The peanuts were warm in long pink bags, and I deliberately turned mine upside down and let them spill, which started my mother crying, weeping really, and assured me that whatever I was sensing was true. In the backseat of a cab she held me on her lap, something she hadn't done for a long time.

We moved into an apartment overtop of Del Luca's Bakery. My mother wasted no time before she had a job cleaning houses, a pompadour dyed red-maroon, and a large man named Cal who worked construction and seemed afraid of me. It was Cal who dropped me off in the schoolyard the morning I met my friend Patrice. Cal drove a loud, brown Pontiac with a yellow-haired mermaid on the hood.

"Knock 'em dead," was what he always said before I slipped out of the car.

That morning, as usual, I walked over to stand by a wall, as if I knew exactly where I was supposed to be. Directly across from me, Patrice stood bouncing a navy blue ball in a shaded stairwell. I watched her for a moment, overcome with the feeling that she was someone I already knew. She turned to look at me with steady eyes, then smiled. Her hair was black, cropped short, untamed. She walked toward me in her light blue dress, bouncing the ball, her presence in a few moments revealing to me the depth of my loneliness as it simultaneously promised to be the cure. We began bouncing the ball back and forth into each other's hands, launching our friendship.

I think there's a kind of absolute receptiveness, born of need, that was the gift my father had left me.

"So how was school?" my mother asked me in the evenings, scanning the want ads with a pen, the radio playing on the windowsill. I'd tell her about Patrice, the most mundane details taking on a kind of mystical significance for me as I spoke. I was sure that what I felt was apparent in facts I could state and puzzled when my mother hardly looked up from the newspaper.

"She had these red and white shoes with buckles. Size two."

"She carries a box of raisins in her pocket."

"She has a doll named Fred who's been to a doll hospital."

My mother might glance over then and say, "Really. So did you learn anything today? Spelling? Numbers?"

"Both."

....

"Well," she finally said one night, "So have your little friend sleep over, why don't ya? I wanna meet this kid." She had never seen me so enraptured, or at least not in a long time.

I didn't want Patrice to sleep over in our apartment. It did not feel like home and, because we were overtop of a bakery, the cramped rooms smelled of bread and grease, which embarrassed me.

We picked her up at her stone house which seemed like a mansion ("Don't mind me," my mother said), the whole yard manicured, a small white birdbath in the center. Patrice stepped out in a baseball cap and carried to the car a small suitcase packed with pajamas, art supplies, favorite rocks. She got into the car and said hello, and my mother turned around and smiled at her, then stared as if slightly disappointed: So this was her? Couldn't my mother *see?*

That evening we climbed out my bedroom window onto the tar roof of the bakery and talked under a tin vent that jutted from the high brick wall above our heads. Eventually we fell asleep under the gushing warmth of rising bread, and when we woke it was dark, much cooler, and she cried at finding herself there. I felt responsible, seeing the place through her eyes—the littered roof, the dingy street below where an old woman in a nightgown called for a dog, the bright quarter moon sharp as a fang over our heads.

I ushered her inside the window, mumbling whatever words of consolation I knew then.

In my bedroom we heard the sound of my mother and Cal screaming at each other down the hall, and she cried harder and said she had to go home right now. I did not try to convince her to stay, but held up things in my room that I imagined would stop her crying—a clown figurine, a doll, a blue music box my father had sent me. Of course this only made her cry harder. I gave up and walked down the hall.

In the doorway I saw my mother on her knees, her arms thrown around Cal's thighs, her face lined against him, her eyes closed. The feeling in the room made my neck burn. I looked at the floor and said, "Stand up. Patrice has to go home."

My mother opened her eyes, rose to her feet, looked at Cal, then looked at me. She brushed off her lap as if there were crumbs all over it. "We'll drive her home, honey. Is everything all right?" She sounded like she might cry, and her face was red. Cal stared out the window.

Back in my room, Patrice was rocking on the bed, suitcase beside her, clothes pulled on recklessly over her pajamas.

We drove her home. In the backseat she and I hugged separate doors and stared out the windows. When I looked to the front seat, I saw my mother turned toward Cal, smiling, her profile facing me like the side of her she didn't know I knew. We reached the stone house and my friend slipped out of the car. I assumed this severing was permanent and would not be consoled.

But the next week I slept at her house—the start of a ritual that would go on for years.

When I couldn't fall asleep there, I spied on her parents who read hardbacked books at night in armchairs by a window. I would sit on the steps and watch them without being seen, my heart racing, my body prepared to run in case one of them got up.

It was her father I watched most closely, her father who took us to the amusement park when we'd least expect it, ride the roller coaster with each of us tucked under an arm, her brothers in the seats behind us screaming, taking full advantage of the only time they were allowed to say "Shit!" and "Goddamn!" Her father in his old, plaid shirts, his arms strong with pronounced veins. I was so shy with him that on the roller coaster my scream remained caught inside of me. I loved the smell of his body.

And it was her father who would watch us from a window in the house as we dug graves in her backyard for one of her deceased pets. She kept enough of them that on any given week one could be counted on to die. Hamsters, fish, turtles, iguanas, mice, guinea pigs, ducks, a dog, two cats, rabbits.

I had always taken it for granted that I loved animals but saw now that I did not. Not like Patrice. After ten minutes of being with them in the basement I'd grow restless and wish we were outside walking the streets of that neighborhood (she called it a village) where we could endlessly talk. I was jealous not of the animals winning her attention, but of her ability to find them enthralling.

Often I'd have to force myself to feel sad at her backyard funerals, the sky itself never failing to conspire with the elaborate ceremony; it would rain, or clouds would thicken and sail toward the sun as we walked up the aisle she'd roped off between trees. She would lower the shoe box coffin into the earth, and then her hands would push dirt into the grave, patting it gently as if even the dirt were a creature to care for. I could see in the periphery her father watching us from a window. And I can still see the dark grass stains on the knees of her red leotards, her serious expression, and her gray suede tie shoes—the only thing she owned that I disliked. To find something associated with her that didn't seem another part of perfection was a relief. It was frightening to love a friend with the sustained intensity of mind I would later direct only to lovers in the first months of passion when the eye, voracious, sees in exquisite, relentless particulars.

I can see those gray tie shoes rising into a blue sky one at a time, heaved with all her strength on one of the days her father took us to a giant trampoline. He knew about such things—his sense of landscape was like a child's would be in a world where children could drive.

You could pay a quarter and jump for hours—an old woman owned it and sometimes walked out of her blue house down the wooden steps and into the field to stand and watch us jump. My friend's father would stop jumping first, walk off into the field, light a filterless Camel and stand there in a plaid jacket looking at the horizon. By now I understood that though he was a loving father, a giving man, he was lonely, unhappy somehow. This deepened my feeling for him, and for Patrice, whose efforts to relieve him of this loneliness were tireless.

Walking away from the trampoline, her face flushed, she asked him questions or told jokes or stories, bouncing around him in half circles, her eyes searching his face. And he always listened, half of him never failing to attend to her. What kept her busy was trying to reach the other half.

Sometimes he scooped her up onto his back or shoulders and ran toward the blue Chevy like a horse. I would walk behind them, a smile on my face, trying to fight off a feeling of sudden isolation. Back at the car her father would give me a loose hug before I got into the backseat. On one of those days, a day that was particularly cold and gray, he told me, unexpectedly, that I was "like his own kid," and he'd adopt me in a second if he could. And though I loved her mother, I took to imagining her finding another man so her father could marry my mother, even though I knew the two of them would never mix.

But Cal was gone now.

"He won't be back," was all my mother said that night at supper when I asked where Cal was. The red formica table looked a lot emptier. Her eyes were swollen from crying, and she didn't look at me. It was the middle of spring, warm breezes making the white curtains dance.

Her makeup was louder than usual after that, and she didn't talk much. If she caught me staring at her she'd say, "What's with you, Cookie-Lou?" her eyebrows arching defensively. She blared Top 40 music on our kitchen radio as if to cover up the birdsong and did exercises with a woman on the TV whose name, I assume, was Gloria, since I often heard my mother in the middle of a sit-up shouting, "Goddamn, Gloria!" or "Tryin' to kill me, Gloria?" But fueled by rage, or fear, or a fine combination of the two, she got herself in shape, as they say.

The following autumn, enter Manuel.

Manuel was the new worker in the bakery downstairs who every night carried day-old cakes and pastries up the iron steps and into our kitchen, whistling—such was his elation. He played the steel drum in the park on Saturdays, had a beautiful Mexican accent, and wore a black felt hat the color of his eyes.

They spent most of their time in her room with the shades drawn. Patrice and I sometimes brought them breakfast in bed on Sunday mornings. We'd cut toast into heart shapes, smear it with strawberry jam, and serve it on a tray, trying not to turn red in the knowledge that the only thing between Manuel's naked body and us were the sheets and a few feet of dim air. He would wink at us and rave over the meal after we left the room at the top of his lungs so we'd hear, "My God, look at these hearts of toast!"

It seems in memory that Manuel was with us for a long time.

"I'll never forget him," my mother said, years later. "He was young enough to be my son, but for five and a half months he made me feel the rest of the world didn't exist."

"Five and a half months?" I said. "And then what?"

"He took a bus to California," she said. "Sent us a bunch of oranges once, in a box of snow."

I remembered those oranges, how she knelt in the kitchen over the box one winter evening, taking each orange out, one at a time, holding it in her hand, staring at it as if it might tell her something, then setting it back into the snow of the box again.

My friend and I had outgrown our dummies by this time; we were too old now to ride them on our bikes. But we kept them around anyway, as if we needed their reproach. To look at them was to be accused of changing, of growing up. We didn't want to do either of those things.

And the silence of our dark fort, which once held only our hushed voices in candlelight, was broken now by our transistor radios, our singing along with Buddy Holly or The Dominoes. We made microphones with our fists, let our hair fall over one eye, imagined an audience—an audience, even an imaginary one, changes everything. The world outside was with us as it had never been before.

It must have been this time when I began shedding parts of myself, consciously losing my own characteristics and taking on hers; I changed my walk first, quite deliberately. I had always walked with my head lowered, my eyes raised, my hands fisted at my sides. I left that walk behind and adopted hers with an ease made possible by the years I'd spent watching her so closely. I not only knew the walk, I knew the spirit one had to muster to inspire the walk. Now I, too, was walking on my toes like an optimist, my head up straight. A teacher in fifth grade noticed and pulled me aside one day in the hall to say, "Walk like yourself. Be yourself."

"I am myself," I said back to her, too quietly, and flushed with shame.

But I didn't return to my old way of walking. I only bounced more deliberately, my arms swinging with great energy at my

....

sides, my hands open. The walk was so violently out of character I felt it as a shocking release.

We began to hear from others how much we looked alike, the way couples do after decades of domesticity. We looked nothing alike. I was tall, too thin, with crooked teeth and small, deeply set blue eyes. She was smaller, graceful, with soft, large eyes and a lively mouth. But everyone, even strangers, thought we looked like sisters.

At school our insularity was never envied.

"Them two are in their own world."

And to me they said: "If she died, would you shoot yourself or jump off a bridge?"

"Jump off a bridge," I'd say, and then the two of us would laugh and wander off. We were prone to fits of laughter then; it didn't take much to send us falling to the ground, holding our sides, our eyes watering, sometimes tears streaming down our cheeks. We could make each other laugh just by looking at each other. It had the intensity, the pleasure pain, of church laughter, or any laughter whose depth is partially a response to confinement, and yet we laughed this way alone in fields miles from the admonishing eyes of others. The laughter would start to die down, then one of us would snort and start the whole thing up again. Finally, when we were fully exhausted, we'd grow quiet and watch the world step forward—a tree, a fence, a house, a stranger across the street—singularities again. Soon we'd get up and walk somewhere, talking, talking.

My mother worked two jobs now—one cleaning offices, the other as a waitress at Nicole's on Fire, a fashionable restaurant two blocks from our apartment. She grew her hair long and let it be streaked with gray. At night she relaxed by drinking herself into a quiet oblivion, often accompanied by a tall, very thin man whom she'd told more than once, "I really like you, but not in that way, that's all." So Johnny slept on the couch. He made us beef stew on Sundays. He always carried with him pictures of his father, not in a wallet, but in a folder. I watched as he explained the pictures to my mother one evening; she laughed like he was telling her jokes, and he smiled through his stories as if willing himself to believe she was laughing *with* him. I pitied him and did not know enough then to pity my mother's cruelty, so I hated her for it. After she fell asleep Johnny and I would sit at the table, sharing a Coke, not saying a lot, as far as I can remember. I remember him staring out the window with a tense jaw and sad, almost black eyes.

Despite my mother's exhaustion and drinking, she managed to notice my vanishing act. "You walk like her," she said one day. "But on you it looks like a wild animal. And your hair worn that way doesn't do justice either. And what the hell do you mean Johnny's a loner in need of tender mercy? You're not *her*, you're you."

My face burned.

"So?" I said.

"And I wish you'd find other friends. It's not healthy."

"What?"

"You don't give each other time to breathe. Worse than Siamese twins. It's not a damn bit healthy."

I ran out the side door, down the iron steps that led to the ground, then all the way to the street's end. I watched a train go by, then wandered across the hot tracks into a lot where a mountain of slag sat for years by a high fence. I didn't know why, exactly, but I was crying for the first time in a long while, and I started to climb the slag heap, as if it could take me away from myself. The slag was black and gray and sharper than rock, and the sky was the blue that hurts your eyes, and I kept staring up at it, as hard as I could. But the next thing I knew I lost my footing and was slipping, falling down the heap, scraping and cutting my legs up. I jumped off of that heap and looked down at my legs, the bright blood running in rivulets.

"Jesus!" my mother said when I walked into the kitchen, "what the hell happened?" She reached up into the cabinet for white swathe bandages and tossed me a cold rag while I tried to explain. She wouldn't look at my legs; blood made her want to pass out.

"Why in the hell would anyone climb a slag heap?" she kept saying.

I washed my legs and wrapped them in bandages while she went and got ready for work. "Are you gonna be all right?" she said in the doorway of my bedroom before she left that evening in her starched white uniform.

My friend's father unwrapped those bandages in Nashville. He had taken us to Tennessee to teach us some history. We all stayed in a Nashville motel one night—her father, brothers, and the two of us—her mother at home with the youngest. He unwrapped the bandages and applied an ointment to my legs from a white tube. He was crouched before me, his face focused and confident that whatever he was applying would heal more quickly than the bandages. Being touched like that, cool ointment up and down my legs, evoked a strange collision of feelings. I could suddenly remember being washed and towel-dried as a very small child, my mother or father crouched before me as he was. And I was simultaneously overpowered: this ointment, this touch, filled me with desire so sudden and consuming I had to cross my arms to keep from grabbing hold of his hair. When a cry escaped me, mostly in confused shock, he thought the ointment had stung me, took his hands away, looked up, and said, "Sorry honey, but if it hurts that probably just means it's working."

Desire turns you, turns your whole body and your world. Everything you've ever heard or read or seen tells you that what's about to happen—your so-called first love—is more important than all the years of friendship preceding it.

I waited, knowing one sort of boy would approach Patrice, and another, if any, would approach me.

John McGrail singled her out. He was popular, athletic, his family had horses, and when my mother saw his school picture she said, "So who's the movie star?" Now when Patrice looked at me her eyes seemed preoccupied, though that was likely her defense against what may have looked like panic in my own.

At the outdoor skating rink she and John were among the couple-skaters skating to blared love songs. She wore a flared red felt skirt with white snowflakes sewn around the hemline. From behind the fence under bright towering lights I watched them. Jean Marie Downing, a homely girl in a coat with a high fur collar, stood beside me. She was so shy she closed her eyes when she spoke to people. Our hands gripped the chain link fence and scared me in their bony, blue similarity.

On the ice John McGrail whispered something in Patrice's ear; she threw her head back and laughed, a habit which so many girls forced then but on her looked genuine. A few times she looked over at me and rolled her eyes as if to assure me she wasn't having that great a time, and I rolled mine back at her, but we both knew this old exchange wasn't working anymore.

And Jean Marie Downing was trying to sing along with "You Send Me," pretending she knew the words by singing them just a split second too late; her voice trailed Sam Cooke's like a groping hand. I wanted to move away from her but made myself stay put. To move away would be to align myself with all those who were moving away from me.

....

I believed that people could look at me now and envision our cramped apartment, my mother drinking in her chair, the rage in her eyes, Johnny's legs hanging off the couch, his unhappy hands clenched on the kitchen table. They could see it in my cheap clothes, my crooked teeth, the look in my eyes.

Patrice skated backwards, hands in white gloves spread on her thighs, John skated forward, following. When the couple skate ended, John's friends—now her friends too—gathered around her and John for a huddle. I could hear her clear laughter rising out of the middle of it. Then a new song was playing and Jean Marie said it was time to skate again. "You go on," I told her.

And before I left that night to take the bus home, I watched Jean Marie skating alone on her long, wobbly legs, her eyes on the ice, her mouth moving as if she were talking to herself. Then Patrice approached her, face devoid of pity. "Hi Jean Marie," she said, then looked over at me. "Come on!" she called, "come skate!" Her hood had come down, her black hair was blown back, and I was suddenly aware of the moon above us. "Come on!" she said again, and looked afraid, as if she knew that on some barely conscious level I was making some sort of decision then to leave her behind somehow, to find another world. For in that world I knew I'd be lost. Even if I'd had what it took to enter it—how, when she demanded all the love anyone could conjure, could there be any left over for me?

I rode the bus home that night and knew for the first time what it meant to be consumed with jealousy. It meant for one thing you deserved whatever was coming your way, if you could be so small as to feel such a thing. I saw a man in the back of the bus with an empty birdcage on his lap talking to himself. It was the first time I imagined myself ending up like that and was strangely comforted by the idea that if things got unbearable I could snap, I could get myself an empty birdcage and talk to myself in the back of a bus.

I looked at my reflection in the window of the bus and heard my mother's attempt to make this time easier. "It's the insides of a girl that really counts," she'd told me.

I declined again and again her invitations to take a walk, to go to her house, to tell her what was wrong. I had no words for what was wrong. *I* was wrong. The closest I could come to explaining was to say I didn't feel well. Her eyes, wounded and confused, were also patient for months. And then, one early spring day after school when I told her I couldn't take a walk by the river, her patience cleared and made way for anger. "Fine," she said, and walked away, calling to a few of her friends, "Hey, wait up!"

It wasn't hard to find another world. It actually found me. I walked down an alley one evening in early June and a car pulled up and blocked the end of the alley like a wall. It was a two-tone aqua and white Chevy. I froze.

The driver, who would've been called a "greaser" back then, leaned out of his window and asked me if I wanted a ride. He said something I didn't understand about how great the car's engine was. Then he was complimenting me, telling me to come closer so he could see my pretty eyes. I walked toward him, smiling at his contrived compliments, blushing and pleased in spite of myself.

"You're so pretty and you don't even know it," he said. Was that what got me into the car? I remember closing the door, my hands settling heavily on my lap like someone else's.

His face was long and thin and pock-marked, almost mournful, and his hair was slicked back, hardened with grease. The car reeked of the Celebrity aftershave that sat on the dashboard.

"Why so shy?" he kept saying as we drove. I had lost my voice. He offered me a toothpick, which I pretended to use, though I'd never used one before. He was busy with one of his own.

We drove through the city listening to the radio, him looking over at me, me looking straight ahead at the road, my heart slamming. Then we were headed toward a freeway ramp, then flying through June dusk on that newly built white road. A song played: *"Johnny Angel, how I love him, and I pray that someday he'll love me, and together we can learn how lovely heaven can be."*

"Where are we going?" I managed to say. By now I had recognized that I was terrified. He was probably nineteen—a grown man. I wouldn't look over at him, I was afraid I'd see his face as a killer's, as one of those men you heard about who went around picking up stray girls so he could cut them to pieces and throw them in the creek.

"I have to go home now," I said, and began to feel I was dreaming.

He took me to a dead-end road facing a valley where people had dumped old furniture, washers and dryers, all kinds of trash. The sky had darkened, save for a thin red rim.

"I have to go home now," I said again.

He turned up the music.

"You're a babe," he said, "Probably fifteen."

"Just turned fourteen."

"No wonder you're scared," he said, "Just relax." He had a voice that sounded unreal, like he was forcing it to be smooth and soft, like another voice lurked underneath of it and might break out any second.

I struggled against him only long enough to know I had no chance. After that, my only protest was a fierce rigidity. He was trying to make the rape romantic, kissing my neck, running his cold finger up and down my inner arm. "Close your eyes," he kept saying, because I held them wide and stared through the windshield.

When I began to cry he held me and kissed the top of my head and said it was always scary the first time, and I remained perfectly stiff as he tore my clothes off and only began to scream when he was inside of me. He put his hand over my mouth and I tried to bite it. "There, baby, there," he kept saying.

Afterwards I cried and shook with rage and shock and a terrible grief. I leaned hard against the window as he drove me back to where he'd picked me up. "Can I call you?" he kept saying, as if he thought this had been our first date. "It's not bad after the first time, you know."

I had him let me off a block from my house. "I'll call you," he said, though I hadn't given him my number. I walked home. I had somehow twisted my neck that night so that for weeks afterwards I had to hold my head bent down to avoid the pain. It was, ironically, the way I'd held my neck before I got rid of my old walk.

I look at Brenda as she grows and count the years she has before her body marks her as a target, an object. As if she's safer now, as a child, when I know it isn't so. Once her father and I, the last year we were together, took her to a lovely park in another city, a place he'd been to as a child. She was five and somehow had managed to wander off, and when I turned to see where she was I saw she was at the side of the road talking to someone in a red car, and I ran for her life, my head and heart about to explode with rage. When I reached her, breathless, I saw a young woman in the driver's seat, a beautiful baby in a yellow hat sitting on her lap, another child in the back. "Is this your little girl?" the woman said. "She's a sweetheart."

When I got back to the empty apartment that night, shaking, my shirt torn, I paced in the kitchen for a long time, crying and trying to think of what to do before I realized I had to take a bath. Of course, a steaming hot bath. As if a rape could be washed away. Afterwards I put on my oldest pajamas, pajamas

....

from childhood. I shook and walked through the rooms and then up and down the hall telling myself out loud the story of what had just happened to me, again and again. An hour or so later I tried to call Patrice. I didn't know what I'd say to her, maybe nothing, maybe I'd just hear her voice and hang up. It was very late, and her father answered. His voice made me realize how much I missed him, but I could not speak. "Hello?" he said again. "Is anyone there?" I tried to say something, anything, but couldn't. Finally he hung up.

The next morning my mother told me she'd had a date but didn't like the man at all. She sat across from me, sunlit in a nightgown at the kitchen table, buttering toast. "All he did was talk about himself," she said. "He never shut up, not even during the movie, and he laughed too loud at all the wrong parts, and then expects afterwards he can do what he wants with me. I don't think he'll be calling again," she said, and laughed.

She was not usually so confiding. I imagined she knew something of what happened to me just by looking at my face. I thought that maybe this was just the way things progressed.

But that night I went down to Nicole's on Fire and watched my mother through a window as she waited on tables. Moving through the dim light, carrying trays on her shoulder, her long hair tied back in a single braid, she looked tired and solitary and more formal than I'd ever seen her. As I watched it grew darker, and though Nicole's was only a block away I was too afraid to walk home, too afraid to leave the lit window of that restaurant. I waited there over four hours until my mother emerged, exhausted, smoking a cigarette, flanked by other waitresses. I had imagined running to her, embracing her, as if we were other people altogether, but now that she was here I was frozen.

"What the hell?" she said when she saw me, but then gave me a one-armed hug, and we were walking home together, and she was telling me a story about one of her demanding customers. "But the tips were good, girl, the tips were good. One of these days you and me are gonna move out of this town and go some place decent and warm."

"We are?" I followed her up the steps into the kitchen.

"Hell yes. What'd you think? We'd be here forever?"

When I was twenty-five years old, living in Seattle, I called Patrice out of the blue and told her I'd be coming to San Francisco. Would she like to have dinner? I made that phone call in a booth outside of a gas station so my apartment wouldn't have to contain the memory of the call—I anticipated the worst.

But she seemed genuinely glad to hear from me. She said she'd like to have dinner.

I took a bus to San Francisco, as nervous and excited as I'd ever been in my life.

In her apartment, guitars and violins were hung all over the wall, and her husband, who made them, answered my questions about them. He was personable enough, but I kept imagining he looked at me with a kind of wariness, a resentment, and felt sure she'd told him the story of my betraying her.

His workshop was in the kitchen's alcove; the rooms smelled of rosewood, and all of them were sunlit. Their new baby, Deirdre, slept in a bassinet next to a bay window. On the wall across from the instruments were photographs, mostly her husband's family, but a few of her own, including one of her father holding Deirdre under a tree. His hair was white, but his expression had not changed. "I bet he's a nice grandfather," I said. She was over on the other side of the room, setting cups of coffee down on the long tiled table.

"He is. He's really great."

"They're coming out to visit us soon," her husband said.

Her husband stayed home with the baby while we took a cable car to Chinatown in and out of fog, both of us in sweaters. We did not meet each other's eyes. We talked fluently about the present: I learned all about her job in a photography lab, how she'd met her husband, what it was like to be a mother, how the only bad thing about their apartment was the rule against keeping animals. Her face, her voice, her way of speaking, had changed only slightly—so slightly I could not have said how. We walked through Chinatown's swarming, dusk-lit streets into a restaurant called the Cave.

We sat across from each other at a table under a huge dragon affixed to the wall above us, and our eyes slowly adjusted to the dark. A waitress came and lit the candle between us. We ordered our dinners, and again, without looking at each other too directly, we took turns talking about our present lives. Despite my discomfort, my pounding heart, talk came easily to us as it always had.

Later, on the Golden Gate Bridge, the lights of the city spread below us, the black water rippling, I stood beside her while she pointed out Alcatraz and told me a brief history of it. Her father had told her, she said. I took that as a kind of cue. "I miss seeing him," I said. "Remember how he'd take us to that old trampoline?" She looked at me, and then down at the water.

"I think so. Was it at an amusement park?"

"No. It was way out in the middle of a field. Remember the old woman who used to watch us jump? The one who owned it?"

She kept looking down at the water. "I have a terrible memory," she said. "But I think I remember the trampoline."

I didn't say anything.

We walked down off of the bridge and then through a park in thick fog where a group of men and women were up on a platform stage singing for a small audience. We looked at them as we headed across the dark ground down a tree-lined path that led to the street.

From the street we could see the Pacific if we stood on a bench and looked over a low wall. We watched the waves for a few moments of what seemed awkward silence to me at the time, and I said I had to be going.

We said the usual things—it was great to see you, keep in touch, we should do it again sometime. And we looked each other in the eye, which seared me.

I never saw the boy who raped me again, save for in nightmares. But the next year another boy, slightly younger, who also had a car that reeked of aftershave, became my boyfriend. We were *going together*. He wore a black leather jacket and didn't talk a lot, but his eyes were warm, and he gave me a ring. I liked how I could make him feel, how he would hold to me breathing as if he wanted to cry. We drank together from a small bottle of rum with a naked woman dancing on the label in a red fur hat. There were a few times when we went to Homer's, a small hamburger place on the highway close to the suburbs, and from the car window I saw Patrice standing with a whole group of people, all of them in soft bright sweaters, shiny hair, straight, perfect-looking teeth. While he went in and ordered us take-out food, I would stay in the car, slumped down in my seat so that if by chance she looked over she wouldn't see me. He'd come back with food and Camels and off we'd drive. He took me home always just after midnight after first taking me to Cecil's Diner, where I could use the bathroom to make myself presentable.

In the apartment my mother would be sitting in the blue chair by the window listening to the radio, relaxing with a drink, her hair up in a towel so that her face, devoid of makeup, was more apparent, vulnerable, older. If she was drunk, one eye would be halfway closed, the other held wide in opposition.

"Sit," she'd tell me. I'd sit on the end of the couch, arms folded.

"Have some fun out there?"

"Yep."

"That's good. This is the best time of your life, ya know."

"I know."

"You'll always look back and think that."

"I know, Mom."

Soon she would close her eyes and rest her head back on the chair like a much older person. It terrified me. She would tell a story, something from when she was my age, how she thought life would always be terrible, but then, then she met my father. At that point her voice would get higher, dreamy, a smile would invade her face. I hated, most of all, her stories of going to carnivals with him all over the East Coast. He loved a carnival, that man, even in the rain. One summer when she was seventeen they did nothing but go to carnivals. They slept under the stars out in fields.

I tried not to look at her as she spoke, but that was impossible.

When she was sick in the hospital with spinal meningitis, that man would not leave the foot of her bed, even to sleep.

When I was born, that man held me and cried like a baby.

He's probably at some carnival now, she said, right now, wandering around with that look on his face, that look. . . .

After she fell asleep I would walk down the hall and run the hottest bath I could tolerate and lie in the water in the dark, everything submerged but my head. I would force myself not to think at this time. Not about the night I'd had, not about the friend I'd lost, not about the future that would someday contain my daughter, who sleeps in the next room, and not about my mother asleep in the blue chair whose delving into the past I could not understand. Any more than I could see that her face was consumed by a kind of forgiveness—of my father, of herself, of whatever had torn them apart—a gift that was hers when she was too tired for truth, which is when, I think, we remember.

PREVIOUS WINNERS OF
THE DRUE HEINZ LITERATURE PRIZE

The Death of Descartes, David Bosworth, 1981

Dancing for Men, Robley Wilson, 1982

Private Parties, Jonathan Penner, 1983

The Luckiest Man in the World, Randall Silvis, 1984

The Man Who Loved Levittown, W. D. Wetherell, 1985

Under the Wheat, Rick DeMarinis, 1986

In the Music Library, Ellen Hunnicutt, 1987

Moustapha's Eclipse, Reginald McKnight, 1988

Cartographies, Maya Sonenberg, 1989

Limbo River, Rick Hillis, 1990

Have You Seen Me?, Elizabeth Graver, 1991